DIAMONDS IN PARADISE

DIAMONDS IN PARADISE

AN ALL ABOUT THE DIAMOND ROMANCE

NAOMI SPRINGTHORP

Nancy,
Rick & Sherry's
story tied up w/a
shiny bow. Watch for Chase 2/19!
Thanks for reading.
Naomi

Diamonds in Paradise

An All About the Diamond Romance

Published by Naomi Springthorp

Paperback Edition ISBN 978-1-949243-05-5

Cover Photographer: Randy Sewell of RLS Model Images Photography

Cover Model: Chris Mayo

Graphic Designer: Irene Johnson johnsoni@mac.com

Editor: Katrina Fair

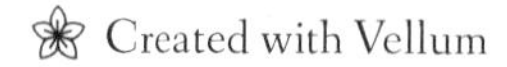

Created with Vellum

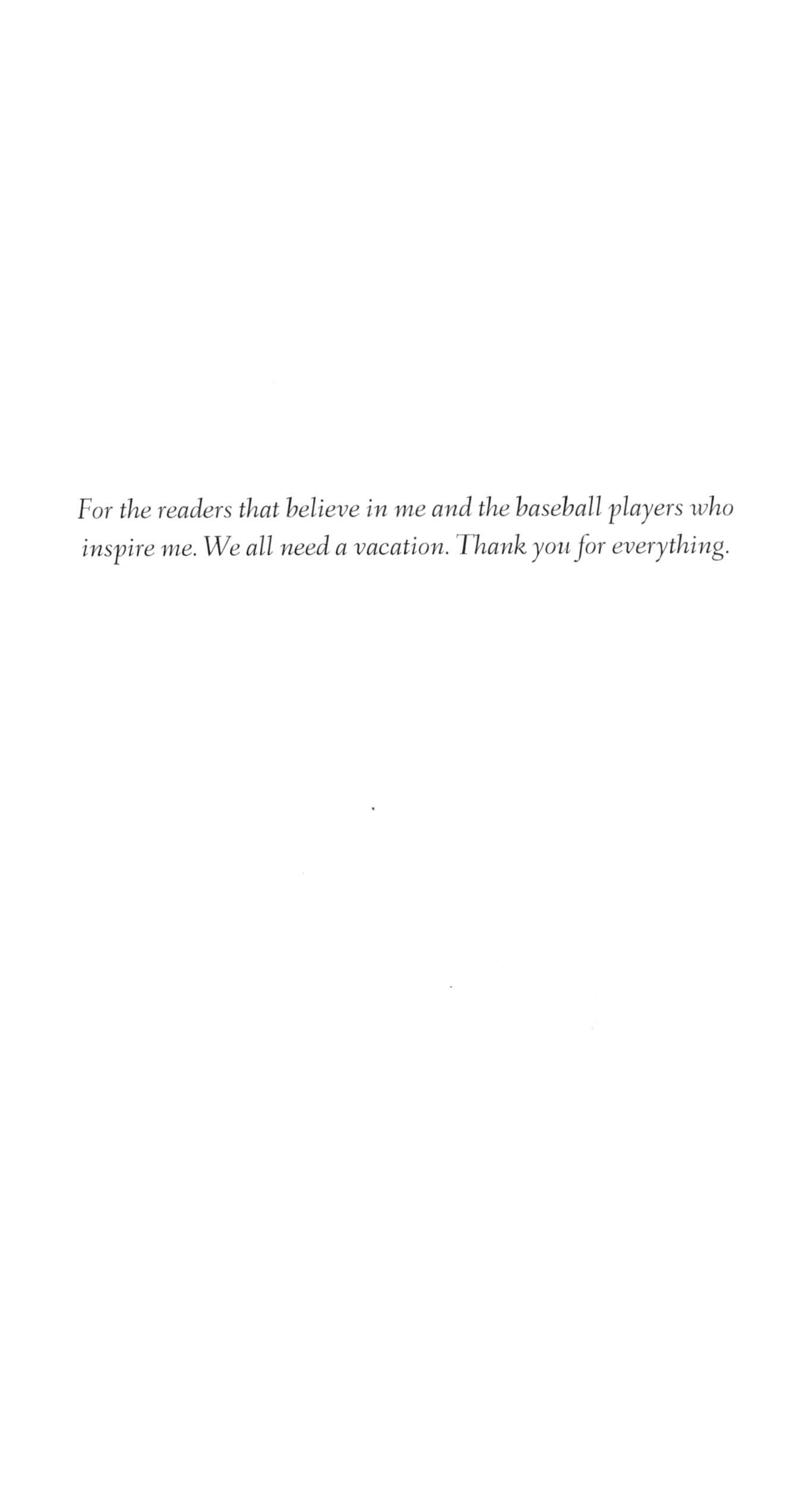

For the readers that believe in me and the baseball players who inspire me. We all need a vacation. Thank you for everything.

CHAPTER ONE

The season was over and Rick's team, the San Diego Seals, made it to the playoffs. Unfortunately, they were knocked out in the first round. I was concerned he'd be grumpy, but it was the opposite. He was content to have free time and be able to rest. He turned into a baseball fan and watched every single playoff game all the way through the end of the World Series. Granted, he's more critical of the players than the average fan and took notes about some of the players, but he's into it. He had a team he was cheering for. It's nice to finally be able to sit together watching baseball and hold hands. Some of the games were watched naked and watched may not be the right word. Let's face it: Some of the games were background noise or noise to cover my, uh, my calling out my king's name.

I was anxious for our trip to Hawaii and had already started packing. My work was caught up, our condo was clean and I'd been dreaming of white sandy beaches with beautiful glassy blue waves. I'd booked us a studio cottage on the sand at the only resort on the North Shore of Oahu for two weeks and I couldn't wait to take Rick to some of my favorite places.

I call the car service to take us to the airport, since I'm a travel agent I'm dubbed the "Vacation Commander". I pull my suitcase out of the closet, packed and ready to go. I pack light because, well, it's Hawaii. What do I really need? Swimsuits, shorts, tank tops, flip flops, tennis shoes, sundresses, panties, bras, beach cover up, my small make-up case with toothbrush, camera, and a sweater in case it gets cool in the evening or to dress up my tank top for a restaurant. I considered lingerie, but considering I won't be wearing much already, it kind of seemed redundant. Rick packed everything and I mean he needed a separate bag for his workout gear. I carry my huge purse with me, so I can keep my laptop, iPod, earbuds, book, magazine, fuzzy socks and snacks with me on the plane. Sometimes my feet get cold on the plane and fuzzy socks are the answer. I packed extra snacks, so I have enough for both of us and even got a splitter for my iPod in case Rick wants to share with me. I'm dressed in jeggings, flip flops, tank top, and my Seals hoodie with Seno and a big 6 on the back for the flight. Rick is wearing jeans, tennis shoes, a snug fitting Seals clubhouse T-shirt screen printed with "Property of the San Diego Seals" across the chest and a short sleeve button up shirt that's probably the closest thing he owns to an aloha shirt. I'm still stuck on the T-shirt. Sometimes Rick simply puts on a T-shirt and I'm reminded my fantasy baseball boyfriend is not only real, but loves me. The snug fit of the shirt showing off his muscles every time he moves, especially the width of his shoulders. Doesn't matter how long it's been, I still get slapped across the face with reality when he introduces me as his fiancé or leaves me something under the name Sherry Seno.

His world of professional baseball is now my world and I'm still adapting. Today as we board the plane and sit in first class for example, I would never have flown first class, but Rick told me to book first class. It's a luxury, like having the private cottage instead of a simple hotel room. It's not what I'm used to, but I'm not complaining.

We get on the plane for our 9am flight and the flight attendant is passing out Mai Tai's to everyone in first class. I realize we've traveled a lot over the last six months going to away games, but never flown together. We focus on each other as we take the drinks and each have a second one before we take off. We don't have to speak, we're in the moment together. I can't tell you much about the flight, but we laughed and kept the flight attendant busy bringing us drinks. I took the snacks out of my bag to share with my man and he shook his head at me, "What else do you have in your bag?" Rick takes my bag away from me and pulls me over to sit in his lap. He gazes into my eyes, "Hi, my queen," and smiles. I want to suggest we join the Mile High Club, but there's no way we fit in that tiny bathroom together. I snuggle into his strong chest as he kisses my forehead and holds me tightly against him. Rick leans his head down against mine and we must fall asleep because the flight attendant wakes us when it's time to land. "Hi, baby. Are you ready for our first vacation together?" Rick asks with a dirty grin and clear blue eyes that remind me of the ocean we're flying over as we come in for landing at Honolulu Airport.

"I like the sound of that. Our first vacation. It means there are many more to come." I smile at my man, unable to contain my happiness as I'm struck again with my amazing reality.

Rick gets a dirty glint in his eyes, "I'm looking forward to making you come many times on this trip." My body hums at his words and I know we're going to spend most of today in bed. Rick claims my mouth with his, taking my breath away with his intent and the flight attendant has to tap him on the shoulder to get me back into my seat for landing.

The sun is shining and the water below us is so clear you can see what's underneath it from the plane. There's a beautiful view of Diamond Head, Waikiki, and Honolulu as we fly in. The landing is easy, and Rick grabs for my hand intertwining our fingers as we disembark.

We're met immediately by a friendly Hawaiian woman who places a lei over each of our heads. Our leis are made of beautiful, fresh, purple orchids. We walk through the airport to the rental car lot and pick up our wheels. I'd reserved a Jeep Wrangler and they had it ready and waiting. I love it when things go as planned. We get our things loaded into the Jeep and climb in. Rick is driving, while I navigate from the shotgun position.

I've been playing this day in my head for weeks, imagining where we'll start and what we'll do. Rick wants to get checked into our cottage, relax and have some time to ourselves, naked. I want to give him everything he wants. I'm excited to see our cottage, I know it'll have a spectacular view. I direct Rick to the freeway, and eventually the gorgeous view of the ocean comes into sight as we drive down the hill toward Kamehameha Highway. I have him take the turn off for Haleiwa and turn right. It's a two-lane road through town and it can be crowded, but it's always worth it. The main road is lined with restaurants, shopping, galleries, shave ice, and mostly locally owned small businesses. I direct Rick to turn right into the shopping center with the general store and the Surfer Grill, then to park off to the side where it's not crowded. I hop out of the Jeep and strip down to the bikini I have on under my clothes. I take off my hoodie, slide my slippahs (I'm in Hawaii now, right?) off, pull my shorts out of my purse, and shimmy out of my jeggings right there in the parking lot. I pull my shorts on and my tank top off, while Rick is watching me the whole time, enjoying the view. My side of the Jeep is hidden to everyone enjoying the shopping center. Rick walks around to me and his eyes heat up instantly. He shakes his head at me telling me how much he's enjoying me changing clothes in public and that he doesn't like to share at the same time, which I didn't even consider being an issue or indecent in any way. But, it did it for Rick. He backs me up against the Jeep, splaying his hands across my bare skin as he presses his lips to mine tenderly, gently sucking on my lower lip as his heat, need, and desire builds. I run my fingers through his hair and my body reaches for his. I slide my tongue in his mouth and he sucks on it. He pulls away from me and feasts on me with dark hooded eyes. I get a big grin on my face and I can't control it, "Soon, my king." I give Rick a quick kiss, grab his hand and drag him into the general store to get us aloha shirts. We laugh as we thumb through the rack, trying different shirts on and finding the shirts we want. I pull him into the Surfer Grill next door, and I know the surf is going off because the service staff is at a minimum. It's a Hawaii thing. If the surf is good, the service probably isn't. Everybody takes off for the waves and leaves the guy with the short straw left at work to cover them. Especially at local places like this. What do you expect from a place that has rafters full of surfboards hanging from the ceiling and big screens playing surfing? The bar has thatching around it and the outdoor tables have thatched umbrellas covering them. The windows run down to the floor and turn open, allowing birds to wander and fly in. We get a table by the window with a view of one of the big screens and the waitress walks up with menus. The waitress is wearing Uggs with cut-off denim shorts and a tank top over her swimsuit which is obviously as wet as her hair is. She's recently back from her lunch break and she spent it surfing. Rick puts his arm around me and I do the ordering since we're in my place. I order a lava flow, a ginger beer, kalua pork fries, and a macadamia nut chicken sandwich.

"Is this how it's going to be? Are you in charge in Hawaii?" Rick grins at me jokingly.

"You started it with the 'Vacation Commander' title." I can't help myself and laugh. "This is one of my favorite places to eat, I love the atmosphere and the food. The resort is only about eight miles from here and the drive is one of the most beautiful that you'll ever experience. We'll stop and explore later in the week, but today we're going to check in and hang out together at our cottage. Unless that doesn't work for you?" I wait for his response.

Rick runs his hand up my leg and leans into my ear, his hot breath on my neck when he whispers, "I'm with you and that makes everything perfect. I love you, my queen." He gives me an open mouth kiss below my ear and it sends shivers all the way to my toes.

The waitress brings our drinks and the fries. The lava flow is served in a coconut cup with an umbrella and the fries are deliciously cheesy, better than I remember. Rick holds my hand under the table and we share the kalua pork fries. The fries are a huge serving, so we also share the sandwich when it arrives. The sandwich is a boneless skinless chicken breast coated in macadamia nuts on a wheat bun. I slurp the last bit of my lava flow and Rick is antsy. We take off for the Jeep and head out to the highway. We drive the seven miles of miracle beaches from Haleiwa to Kahuku, passing Waimea Bay, Sunset Beach, Sharks Cove, Three Tables, Goat Island, Ehukai State Beach, Banzai Pipeline, and unbelievable ocean views the whole way.

CHAPTER TWO

We arrive at the resort and pull up to the valet who greets us with shell leis. Rick and I walk into the open lobby area and get checked in quickly. We're introduced to our personal concierge, Alika, who has already loaded our bags onto a golf cart. He gives us a quick tour of the lobby, shows us where the pool is, where the restaurants are, and points out the gift shops. We get in the golf cart and our concierge drives us along a pathway through lush tropical gardens with huge palms and birds of paradise to the cottages. Alika stops at our cottage, unlocks the door for us and carries our bags into our room. The cottage is appointed with Hawaiian woods and patterns, everything is luxurious. He shows us how to work the lights and the big doors out to the beach, leaving us a number we can reach him at if we want anything. He leaves the big doors open giving us an amazing view of the waves rolling into the shore and pulls down the privacy screen, so we can take pleasure in the beauty of the ocean and each other.

Rick simply smiles at me and we're drawn together like

magnets. His hands on my hips, standing a few inches apart with him gazing into my eyes, "I can't wait for you to be Sherry Seno." His low, wanting voice cuts straight through me.

"I'm yours already. Only you, Rick." We lean into each other and kiss. Our connection controlling my heartbeat, it's all consuming and nothing else exists. I need to get closer to him, I need him inside me. I unbutton his jeans and he slides my aloha shirt off of my shoulders, tossing it across the room. I push his jeans down, releasing his hard cock. He toes off his shoes and tosses his shirt aside as he leads me to the huge king bed. I sit on the edge of the bed and find my position perfect to lick his length, I swirl my tongue around his tip and taste the moisture there. I draw a manly groan from Rick and he takes over, pushing me down on the bed. He crawls up over me, laying between my legs with his weight on me and presses his lips to mine sweetly. Rick wraps his arms around me, holding me and kissing me, and kissing me, and kissing me. I feel his cock at my hot wet sex and he slides into me deliciously while he continues to kiss me. Slowly moving in and out, filling me and then taking it away. Both of us shiver at our connection. "I love you, my king. We belong together."

"Yes, my queen. We belong together." He moves his magic lips to my neck with a trail of kisses as he continues to move in and out, deliberate and slow. He moves his hands to my breasts, feeling my nipples pebble and squeezing them. I drag my fingers across his shoulders and wrap my legs around his waist as I arch into him. I need him. I need more of him. I want him to know. He lets out a low groan and moves his mouth to my breasts, sucking my nipples as he pushes in and holds himself deep inside of me.

"Oh, Rick!" I can't help but to call out to him.

"That's right, baby. I'm right here. Do you want more? Tell me what you want, my queen." He says evenly.

"More. All of you, my king. I want all of you." Rick pushes in further and I about lose my mind. "My king, oh, my king!" I buck uncontrollably and he holds me down, not willing to give up control.

"Not this time, my queen. I want it to last." He pulls out of me and kisses a trail down my body until his mouth is almost on my sex, "I'll always take care of you," he licks circles around my clit and sucks at it hard while he slides a finger into me. He feels me start to come and buries his face in my wet sex, licking and sucking me senseless.

I see nothing but darkness with bursting stars as I scream out words I don't comprehend. He continues his licking with one hand under my ass and the other spread across my bare stomach.

Rick moves back over me and slides his hard length into me, "You say the sweetest things to me, baby. I love you." Yet again, I don't know what I said. I really need to start recording myself all the time. He continues with his deliberate strokes and his cock is rock solid. He feels so good stroking me, it's incredible. He's incredible. I'm on the outside watching and listening as I hear myself start to whimper with every stroke, and call out his name. It pushes him faster than he wants and he can't help it. I meet his strokes and he moves faster. I reach for his face and pull him to me to kiss him. I press my lips to his, licking across his lips and sliding my tongue against his in time to his stroking in and out. Suddenly I'm on the edge again and he pulls me over with his loud cry muffled by my mouth as he strokes in hard a few times and collapses on top of me, still kissing me. "I love you, baby. All you need to do is tell me when." Rick puts his arms around me and rolls over, bringing me with him and keeping me on top of him.

When what? What did I say? The things I say when I'm sleeping are honestly how I feel and the truth. I wonder about what I say during sex? Do I ask my Rick what I said? Last time I asked him what I said when I was sleeping he told me that I'd tell him when I was awake within a few days. Hmmm... I wonder if I did? Maybe I have a disease and I say the things I want to say, but block myself out from them because I'm actually afraid of the words or the response I'll get to the words. I guess I'll say it coherently sometime in the next few days.

CHAPTER THREE

I wake up a couple hours later still on top of Rick with his arms around me and a blanket pulled up over us. Rick's face nuzzled into my hair. I move to get up, but he holds me to him tightly and caresses my back. It's a feeling I'll never forget, this feeling of being needed, wanted, and loved. He'll do anything for me, and I can't think of anything I've ever been more confident about in my life or anything that meant near as much to me. I touch his chest with my hands, flat palmed and kiss it. His heart beating strong gives me strength to ask. "Rick, earlier you said to tell you when. When what?"

Rick opens his eyes, "Are you serious?"

This is crazy, I shouldn't be, "Yea. I think it's like when I say sweet things to you in the morning before I wake up, which means whatever I said is the truth. But, I don't have a clue what I said." I press my lips together and roll them in, nervous for the response because Rick's body already responded and it's not happy. "Please tell me what I said."

Rick let me go and rolled to his side, so he could focus and read my eyes, "You said you want to get married here."

"And you said to tell you when?" I question him.

"Yes."

"I assumed you'd want to have a wedding in the off season next year, so we'd have time to plan it." It makes sense to me, it takes time to plan and order and reserve locations.

"I just want to be married to you, Sherry. I don't want a big wedding. I want you. This is your favorite place and the scenery is incomparable, we should get married here. If it makes you happy, it makes me happy. I want you to have everything you want. If you want to get married in Hawaii, that's what we'll do." Rick puts his heart on his sleeve for me.

"So, you're thinking maybe we should get married while we're here on vacation? Before we go home two weeks from now? Just us? No family or friends or anything? Is that too quick? We haven't been engaged very long." I ask too many questions and need to shut up. I need to control my DOTM.

Rick smiles at me from his eyes and almost giggles, "Actually, you said we should get married while we're here. It was your idea. I'm sure we can get the few people who matter here in a short amount of time. Most importantly, there's been no one else for me since I first held your hand in mine at the Locale and as far as I'm concerned you can't be Mrs. Rick Seno soon enough. There's no one else who compares to you, Sherry. It will always only be you." He leans his forehead against mine and kisses me sweetly.

I'm completely lost here. Caught off guard. No idea what to do. It seems so fast. And, I did this to myself. Then again, why make another trip to get married when we can do it now? Am I going to be Mrs. Rick Seno? I need a reality check. This can't be my life. Seven months ago the catcher for the Seals, number 6 Rick Seno was the star of my dreams, clean and dirty. He was my fantasy baseball boyfriend and I couldn't get his autograph to save my life. I loved to watch him play with an unmatched intensity on the field. I daydreamed about what it would be like to get to meet him, what I would say. I hung around after the game to watch the on field interviews and wait for my chance to get the couple of autographs I was missing. One night after the game I got lucky getting Cross' autograph and told him I needed Seno's, but went all starry-eyed when Seno was right there doing his on field interview and Cross worried something was wrong with me. Fast forward a couple hours and I'm meeting Seno at the bar, screwing everything up, being tongue tied, saying the wrong thing, lying and somehow still making out with Seno in the back corner booth. Now, I never want to be apart from him because we did that and it was heartbreaking. He's already moved in with me and my life has never been better. I turn the crown engagement ring he gave me around my finger, it shines at me as if it's the shooting star I'm waiting for to wish on. I turn to Rick, "Want to go for a sunset walk with me?"

He smiles and jumps up to change. We get unpacked and go out for a walk around the resort, hand in hand. I'm sure we're annoying to everyone around us, with our huge smiles and arms constantly around each other. The view is breathtaking, but not holding my attention that's centered on the man with his arm around me who wants to marry me and the consideration of getting married while we're in Hawaii. It's unexpected, which is out there because I was sure I'd considered everything we'd do on this trip ahead of time and getting married while we're here is apparently my idea! I'm scared, but the more I think about it, the more I want to do it. Can we do this? It's a dream come true. First my Rick and now marrying him in my favorite place? It's so spontaneous. I smile all the way into my cheeks and my face gets warm all over, happiness at the thought of marrying my Rick, my king.

We stop at the edge of the ocean facing the sunset and I'm leaning back against Rick's chest, his arms around me, holding me. There's a musician playing at the pool bar, just him with his guitar and microphone. He's a local and he's been playing mostly Hawaiian, folk, or Hawaiianized music. I feel Rick's smile at my ear while we watch the sunset's colors change to pinks and shadowed purples with the line of sunlight peaking out around the edge of the clouds. The wind is moving the clouds along, breaking them up into smaller puffs and they look like baseballs rolling across the sky. The guitarist finishes *Somewhere Over the Rainbow* by Iz and starts in on something that sounds familiar. That's it! Every sign that could possibly be thrown at me has appeared. Rick turns me to him and we dance right there on the grass at the edge of the water with the waves crashing. His eyes are locked with mine and he smiles, inspired to dance by the guitarists rendition of "Thinking Out Loud" by Ed Sheehan, our song.

I gaze into his eyes, "When," and his smile actually grows.

He picks me up and swings me around, "Let's do it, my queen. I love you. Let's get married." Rick calls the cocktail server over and asks for champagne to celebrate.

"Hawaiian style?" She asks and he nods at her with no doubt.

He kisses me and swings me around again. I'm not sure I've ever seen him this happy, and my face hurts because I can't stop smiling. This is the right thing to do, more importantly it's what we want to do. I lean my face against his chest, "I love you with all of my heart."

The cocktail server brings us two Blooming Champagne Cocktails that look fancy and exotic. It's a preserved hibiscus flower in the bottom of a champagne flute with champagne poured over it. The flower appears to be blooming and the red tone makes the petals look like flames. Perfect. Rick clinks his glass to mine, "To our forever." I love the effervescence of the champagne, it tickles my nose. We both take a drink. He takes my glass away and sets them both down, freeing our hands. He takes my face in his hands, brushing my hair back and puts his lips on mine, kissing me sweetly. He moves his hands to the back of my head and the small of my back as his kiss becomes claiming, he dips me as he kisses me. The kiss is long and flutters in my gut more than any of Rick's don't-forget-me kisses. When he breaks the kiss and brings me back upright, the crowd of people watching the sunset around the pool bar cheer and clap. Rick all smiles responds to them, "We just decided to get married while we're here. I can't wait for this beautiful woman to be my wife." I blush uncontrollably, my whole body buzzing. We stand together watching the sunset and finish our champagne in silent happiness.

CHAPTER FOUR

We walk back to our cottage and Rick orders room service for a light dinner on our lanai overlooking the ocean. The shine from the stars, moon, and resort dancing off the water's surface. The occasional sea turtle pulling itself out of the ocean onto the sand or poking it's head up out of the water like a periscope. The resort pool glowing in the distance. The time difference and long, eventful day has made us ready for an early night in. We spend the evening talking and making out like teenagers, until we go inside and close up the cottage for the night. We make love for hours with the sound of the ocean roaring in the background and fall asleep in each others arms.

I wake up the next morning confused and I don't know where I am. Something is different, similar to the feeling I had several months ago when I found I had my fantasy baseball boyfriend in bed with me. I hear the sound of the ocean and Rick's arms are wrapped around me, I remember we're on vacation. Then it hits me... We're getting married! I roll over to snuggle my face into Rick's chest to find he's already awake. "Good morning, my queen. You make me happier than I've ever been. How do you feel about ordering breakfast in?" Rick talks into my hair.

I breathe deeply, relaxed and happy to be in my favorite place with my man, my protector, my true love. "Order macadamia nut French toast please, and coffee, and maybe some tropical juice. Ask how long until it will be here. Maybe we can get wedding stuff planned over breakfast. I want to have our vacation time, too." I read his expression, not wanting to be too pushy.

He gives me a cheeky smile, "Sounds good." He goes to order room service and I turn on the shower. "Room service will be here in thirty minutes," Rick calls out.

I walk up to Rick and take his hand, pulling him to the shower with me. We're both still naked from last night and I put my arms around him, pulling him under the shower spray with me. Water dripping over both of us, I watch the droplets build up and run over the tip of his nose once his hair is soaked. I open the small tropical shampoo the resort has supplied and squeeze some into the palm of my hand. I run my hands and fingers through Rick's hair, massaging his scalp and washing his hair. He takes the shampoo and repeats the same thing on me, his hands are magic even when they're simply rubbing my head. We stand under the shower and rinse. He shampoos his beard and I soap up his body from his neck down to his toes, it's an enjoyable journey of touching his body all over, feeling his muscles and admiring my favorite parts. I soap up from my breasts down to my thighs and rub against him, spending some extra time soaping up his now hard cock and drawing a low guttural groan from my man. Rick kisses me roughly and holds my head to his, taking control. I stroke his soapy hard length and enjoy his possessive handling. When he breaks the kiss, I whisper in his ear, "You know the problem with staying in the cottage is there's no elevator. What would you do if we were on an elevator?" His eyes flare and I turn away from him quickly, bending over in front of him.

He grabs my hips without hesitation and pulls me to him. His tip is at my entrance and he stops. "That's not what you'd do if we were on an elevator. You can't keep your hands off me and you wouldn't. You'd slide your dick into me and fuck me hard. I'm so wet for you. Don't you want to fuck me?" He doesn't say a word. He slams his hard length into me all the way and pounds into me over and over, as he digs his fingers into my hips and slides me over his dick, using me to stroke himself. I love it and he's amazing. I scream out, "You're my king, baby. Take me. Take me." He continues to slam into me, in and out, in and out. I'm blindsided by my orgasm and he grabs me before I fall over from the force of it. He immediately follows me over the edge, both of us moaning in ecstasy as he slows and rides us through.

He pulls me up to him and holds me against his solid body, "You drive me crazy sometimes, fucking out of control." He turns me and kisses me, "I love you and everything about you." The water sprays over us while we have our moment, making it our own private space. There's knocking at our door and Rick quickly rinses off, grabs the hotel robe and puts it on as he makes his way to the door. I finish showering and pull on a pair of denim short shorts with a lime green camisole style tank top.

I find Rick on the lanai with breakfast and changed from the robe to a pair of board shorts with no shirt. Fuck me! He's so hot shirtless! I won't manage to get anything done today, well, other than him. His board shorts riding low on his hips. No shirt covering his eight pack of abs and his strong chest. Seeing the muscles in his chest and shoulders move distracts me, he's fucking sexy! I walk up to him on the lanai and put my hands on his chest. He smiles at me and I reach around his neck, pulling his mouth down to me so I can taste him. What is it that makes him undeniable in shorts and no shirt? Who am I kidding? He shows a bare arm and I'm ready to jump him.

Alika walks up to our lanai, "Aloha! Ho'omaika'i 'ana! That's congratulations in Hawaiian. I heard you decided to get married while you're here and thought you might want some assistance."

Rick turns to me and I wonder if Alika's a mind reader. "Yes, please! Does the resort have a minister? How do we reserve him? When is he available?" I stop before I ramble out another dozen questions.

He smiles, "We need to reserve the space at the resort and the minister. How many people will be there and do you need rooms for them?"

Rick answers, "About a dozen people. We will needs rooms. It would be great if we could book a time maybe a couple days before we are scheduled to check out." He looks to me for affirmation and I nod.

"Let me go check the schedule and availability," and he was off to the main hotel to do research for us.

I'm making a list, "We'll need to drive over to Honolulu to get a marriage license, but that's fine. I wanted to take you over to that side of the island exploring one day anyway. I need to visit my friend at the gift shop today, she'll know where to get a dress and things like that I need. Do you think Sam will be my Maid of Honor?"

"She'll love that. I'll call Cross to be my Best Man. We should book the spa and salon for you ladies, too." He tenderly runs his hands up and down my arms. "I want this to be perfect for you, for us. I don't want you worrying about spending money. I want you to have everything." His tone said it all. He wants me to have everything and he means it. I'm giddy and can't help, but to laugh like a schoolgirl. We sit together on the same lounge chair and enjoy some breakfast together. I love everything with macadamia nuts, even the coffee tastes better here.

Alika comes back and catches us making out on the lounge chair, "How about ten days from now at sunset and I can have you set up at the edge of the ocean with the sunset behind the minister?"

Rick and I lock eyes anxiously, then turn to Alika, "Yes!" at the same time. It's the perfect option.

"I'll reserve the time for you. Please get me details on how many rooms as soon as you can. We have availability then, so it shouldn't be a problem."

"Thank you, can you book the spa for my bride that day please. Everything she'll want. Also, book a second spot for her Maid of Honor to go with her." Rick looks to Alika waiting for confirmation.

"I'll do that right now, please let me know if I can help with anything else. I'll check in with you tomorrow." He walks off toward the spa.

Rick gazes at me with a happy grin and dials out on his cell phone, "Hi. Here's Sherry, she wants to talk to you." He hands me his phone.

"Hello?"

"Hey! What do you want to talk to me about?" It's Sam.

I squeal like a child, "I'm getting married in Hawaii, in ten days and I want you to be my Maid of Honor. Will you please?"

You could hear Sam scream without the phone all the way from her home in Colorado, "Yes! I'm honored and I wouldn't miss it!"

"Yay! I'll be sending you flight information later today and a boarding pass the day before the flight. I'll text you the details. Oh, don't tell your parents because he didn't call them yet."

"You two are crazy and I love it! Talk soon!" and she was gone.

Rick calls his parents, while I call my Mom. His father was happy and anxious to get to Hawaii, while his mom hemmed and hawed about us getting married so fast and not having the ceremony in a church.

"Hello? Is everything okay? Why are you calling me while you're on vacation?"

I laugh, "Everything is fine, Mom. Better than fine. I want you to come to Hawaii."

"You know I don't like to travel alone."

"Bring someone with you because I'm marrying Rick!"

"I saw the way he looked at you. I know he'll take care of you. Are you sure about this?"

"I don't need anyone to take care of me." I stop myself, "Mom, I love him and I can be me with him."

"Do it. I'll be there. I wouldn't miss it for the world."

"Thanks, Mom."

"I want you both to be happy. Now, get off the phone and go enjoy your vacation with your husband to be," she laughs.

"Aloha." My mom is ecstatic, with some trepidation about traveling by herself and she's going to find a friend who wants to join her on the trip.

CHAPTER FIVE

Rick needs to work out and call Cross, so I take the Jeep keys and drive to the North Shore Gift Shop in Haleiwa to visit my friend Malia. I love the drive from Kahuku to Haleiwa. It's green and lush, with the ocean at your side. The trees hang over parts of the two-lane highway and there's a bike path on the beach side for sections of it. Some of the beaches have parking lots, while others find people pulling onto the dirt at the side of the road and hoping they don't get stuck there. It's almost all residential and beach, with a few businesses spattered in between. No chain fast food or anything franchised, the one grocery store with a coffee place inside, the local bakery, a couple of cafes, and food trucks parked wherever they find a spot. There are a couple of places where fresh fruit stands pop up occasionally and surf, swim, snorkel equipment rentals are available in the more popular beach areas. I pass Sharks Cove and the grocery store, then Saints Peter and Paul Mission as I approach Waimea Bay. I take the curve slowly and drive the cliffside road with the panoramic view of Waimea Bay. The highway quickly turns back inland through a residential stretch until I see the

Haleiwa surf sign and turn right, passing Haleiwa Beach Park as I head toward the Rainbow Bridge and the souvenir shop my friend Malia runs with her family. I've known her for years and she's part of Hawaii to me. I turn onto the side street, park and hop out of the Jeep.

I stop and look around at all the green, the overgrown grassy areas, the ocean birds, the wild chickens, the canoes, the surfers and the wannabe surfers. Hawaii is all about taking time to enjoy —the view, the ocean air, food, friends, and love. I guess Hawaii is love for me, it's the Aloha State and aloha means love, affection, compassion, mercy in Hawaiian.

I walk up to the gift shop and see Malia's sons cleaning while her daughter sits singing and playing "I'm Yours" by Jason Mraz on the ukulele. She's awesome and gets better every time I hear her, so I stop to listen. "She's getting good, huh?" Malia had walked up next to me without me noticing. I turn to her and give her a hug. "This isn't the time of year you usually visit."

"I have news." I smile uncontrollably. "I got engaged over the summer and we're getting married while we're here."

"I'm so happy for you! But, that doesn't tell me why you're here in November." Malia always wants the facts.

"My Rick is a professional baseball player and he wanted to take me on a vacation as soon as it was his off-season. Last night, we decided to get married while we're here. We flew in yesterday and we're here for two weeks."

"I like to see you happy, my friend. You deserve every happiness. Is he with you?" Malia looks around.

"I want you to meet him and this was supposed to be a completely social visit, but I'm hoping you might be able to help me with a few things for the wedding. I left him at the cottage to do his work out. You'll know exactly what I need, will you help me?"

"Of course! What can I do?"

"I need a dress for me and for his sister, my Maid of Honor. I need flowers and leis. I need Hawaiian traditions. I need music, but I may have found it. Can your daughter play 'Thinking Out Loud?'" Wouldn't that be perfect?

"What sizes?" Pia finishes playing. "Pia play 'Thinking Out Loud' for Sherry." Malia is all business.

Text to Sam - What size dress do you wear?

As I'm texting, Pia starts playing and it's perfect. I video record her and send it to Sam.

Text from Sam - Size 9
Text from Sam - Who's that girl?
Text from Sam - She's playing your song!
Text from Sam - She's great!
Text to Sam - My friend Malia's daughter
Text to Sam - Wedding music?
Text from Sam - Yes Yes Yes
Text to Sam - Don't tell Rick

I turn to Malia, "Will she play for my wedding? It's a paying gig."

"Pia, you want a paying gig playing at Sherry's wedding?" Pia lights up and nods. "You need to have a ring blessing, Ti Leaf and Lava Rock Ceremony, leis for everyone, special leis for the wedding party, flower garland for your hair. White dress for you, tropical print for Maid of Honor, white for the groom with a colored sash, white for the best man with a tropical print is okay. I will make sure the music is good. 'Thinking Out Loud' is your song?"

"What would I do without you? Yes, it's our song." I smile and daydream about my Rick.

Malia laughs, "You've got it bad, girl!" Don't I know it! Before I met Rick I was happy being an independent single woman. Now, I'm not happy if I'm not with him. I never imagined I'd be in this place in my life, wanting to share my life with a man and get married.

My phone vibrates.

Text from Rick - I miss you my queen.

I reply quickly.

Text to Rick - I'm in Haleiwa. I'll be back soon. I miss you, too, my king.

I've been gone a couple of hours and need to get moving. "I have to get back to the cottage. I'll bring him by to meet you tomorrow."

"I can't wait to meet him. What are your sizes? I have an idea and I'll have a couple of dresses for you to see tomorrow. I think I know exactly what you want."

I give Malia the sizes and Alika's phone number at the resort. Malia gives me a phone number to her friend who makes leis. "I want to get Pia a dress to match my Maid of Honor, too."

"Don't worry! Everything will get done. This is Hawaii, no stress. Go back to your man and bring him by to meet me tomorrow." Malia hugs my neck and sends me off.

I take off for the Jeep and wish I had something to take back to Rick, then I realize I'm taking him me.

I pull up to the valet and Alika is waiting for me with the golf cart to take me to the cottage. Malia already called him and he set up the ring blessing, the Ti Leaf and Lava Rock Ceremony and made arrangements for Pia and her ukulele. I tell him I'm a travel agent, in case he needs travel arranged for anybody.

CHAPTER SIX

I walk into the cottage and find Rick napping. Fresh from his after work out shower and wearing only a robe. I climb onto the bed and crawl up him, thinking about abusing his cock with my mouth. But, it can't be like that every time. I keep climbing and gently place my lips on his while I run my fingers through his damp hair. In no time his arms are around me and his smile is against my lips. I nuzzle my face into his neck and kiss him there. "Beach, pool, adventure or sex?" I ask at his ear.

Rick rolls me off of him and postures over me on all fours. "I let you out of the house in these shorts without me? I'm a fool!" He squeezes his hand up my shorts to feel my ass and slides his thumb into my wet folds unexpectedly. I cry out and move against him. He unbuttons my shorts and pulls them off to find my "Eat Me" panties. He pulls them off and takes their suggestion, immediately burying his face in my wet heat. Licking and sucking at my folds, he slides a finger in and moves to circle my clit with his tongue. I reach for his head to hold him there and grind against his tongue. What's come over me? I can't help myself. He sucks harder and nibbles at my folds, driving me absolutely crazy. He groans against me, adding vibration to the attack on my senses. I whimper and call out his name. Rick takes his mouth away and stays very still. "Maybe this is too much for you. I better stop." He's sitting up and watching me.

"No! Please, my king. Please, more!"

"No, you've had enough."

What the fuck? I've had enough? I have not! I want more! I'll know when I've had enough. This has to be a game. I can wait him out. Or... "You're right, I've had too much. Best to stop. Thank you for looking out for me." The expression on his face is priceless, my response was unexpected. I sit up and he pulls back. I get up and start to walk toward the bathroom with a sway to my hips, he can't resist my hips and I'm half naked.

He reaches for me, placing his hands on my hips from behind me, "Where are you going?" His large warm hands caress my hips slowly, lovingly, with heat and desire.

I don't play games with Rick because that's not what we're about and he's been played before. I'm tempted to right now, he's teasing me. I turn around to find him sitting on the edge of the bed naked and drop to my knees to worship at his hard dick, but he stops me. "That's not what I have in mind." He brings me up to my feet and wraps his arms around me as he sits back on the bed as far as he can while still being able to keep his feet on the ground. His mouth at the same level with my breasts, he pulls my top off over my head, unhooks my bra and sends it flying. I kneel on either side of him, my body plastered against his as he runs his hands down the sides of my body. I slide down his body and mount his cock, moving on him slowly as he squeezes my breasts and kisses every part of my body he can get to. The heat is palpable, I let the temptation of teasing him go and enjoy the ride. Hot, sweaty and breathing hard within seconds, I reach for his lips with mine and our connection is complete as he slides his tongue into my mouth.

Both of us on the edge, I hold his face in my hands, pull my mouth away from him and lock eyes with him. I'm emotional and feeling everything, including regret for the thought of playing with him. "You're the only one for me. My only true love. I only want to be with you for the rest of my life. I'll never play games with you. I'll always love you. I want to give you everything. I want to be your everything. I never want to be without you." Rick wraps his arms around me and leans his head against me, holding me.

He gazes up at me, "You're my happiness, my love, my everything." Tears stream down my face. He pulls my lips to his and kisses me sweetly, tenderly with his open mouth. I meet him emotionally and we make out until I start moving on him again. Sliding my body up and down on his hard length slowly. Drawing low groans and cries from him, "Oh, baby. You're so tight on me, you... ggrrrrr..." His hands move to my hips, it's a sign and he's ready. He guides me to exactly what he wants with his gentle touch, increasing the speed I'm stroking him and adding a slight grind with my hips. I know the pattern, it's what does it for him and I'm not arguing. The grind is rubbing my sensitive nub and pushing me faster. His mouth on mine moves to my neck, where he kisses and sucks lightly until I'm on the edge and he pushes up into me hard, biting my neck at the same time and sending me over the edge. He holds me up as I scream out his name and he pumps into me a few times before he follows me over the edge. He falls back onto the bed, taking me down on top of him. I lay there on him, with my head on his chest listening to his heartbeat, his pulse racing, mine matching his.

CHAPTER SEVEN

Rick falls asleep and I get up, letting him rest. We're on vacation and that's what it's for, relaxing. I take advantage of the time to quickly check on work. Everything is good, but I do have a couple emails to take care of and some airfare to book.

First, an email from Rick's dad:

Sherry,
I'd like to bring the Mrs to Hawaii a few days before the wedding. Sooner is better. We don't have to be where you are, we can join you the day before the wedding. Can you help me with this?

Thank you,
MrSeno

I send him a reply...

Mr. Seno,

I'm happy to help you with this. Here are a couple of options, please keep in mind you're wanting to do this on short notice causing the price to be higher than expected.

Option 1 $3,250
1 Week in North Shore Resort Hotel
Roundtrip airfare for 2
1 Week of Rental Car – Jeep Wrangler
Lei Greeting for 2 at the airport
Add upgrade to First Class Airfare +$780
Add Oceanside couples massage +$240
Add Surfing Lessons $200/person

Option 2 $1,885 +
3 Nights in North Shore Resort Hotel
Roundtrip airfare for 2 to Oahu
3 Days of Rental Car on Oahu - Jeep Wrangler
Lei Greeting for 2 at the airport
+++Options for Second Location+++
1. Lanai $2,100 (Quiet, Luxurious, Small Island)
4 Nights Lanai Sweetheart Rock Beach Spa Resort
Roundtrip airfare for 2 hop to Lanai
Lei Greeting for 2 at Lanai Airport
Lanai Transportation Fee for 2
Add Lanai excursion package +$200-$500
2. Maui $1,985 (Resort Area, Close to Shopping, Tourist Island)
4 Nights Kaanapali Hotel
Island airfare hop for 2
Lei Greeting for 2 at Kahului Airport
4 Days Rental Car on Maui - Small SUV
3. Waikiki $1,100 (Beautiful beach in the city, near shopping, party zone)
4 Nights at the Grand Village
4 Additional Days of Rental Car Oahu - Jeep Wrangler

I'm happy to provide more options based on your needs. I'm personally familiar with all of the locations I have offered to you. In my opinion, Waikiki is only good for more than one visit if you want to party it up and go dancing every night. Maui has lots to see if you are interested in exploring. Lanai is simple, relaxing and a unique experience.

Please let me know what you think and feel free to call me.

Aloha,
Sherry
Beach Vacations

Second, an email from Cross:

Hey Sherry,

A few of the guys on the team want to go to the wedding and we want to get there a couple days early. If you don't mind we'd like to take Seno out for kind of a last night with the boys and get him wasted. It's part of my job as Best Man and he doesn't know, so shhh! Promise no girls, it would be a waste on him anyway. If you're good with that, we want to get there two days before the wedding and stay for four nights. Can you get us rooms at the resort and airfare? We can share rooms and will need transportation to the resort. Total of eight of us, so four rooms is good. Quote us first class for the airfare.

Oh! Congrats!

Thanks,
Chase

I love how the kid wants to do what's right and take care of Rick the way a Best Man should. He deserves a Bachelor Party. I check the vacation rentals for the resort to see if they have any villas available the days the team wants to be here and reply to Cross.

Chase,

A Bachelor Party will be fine, but I need him to be functioning the next day!

Roundtrip First Class Airfare to Oahu is $1,190 each (Limited availability the dates you are traveling)

4 Nights in the North Shore Resort Hotel $1,200 per room

But, I found another option for you that may be better. There's a villa available for the days you are looking for with 4 bedrooms and sleeps 12 at $500 per night. Plus, it would give you room to party and the villas have their own pool and hot tub area.

For transportation, you can rent two vehicles for a total of $390, use a car service for about $300 or helicopter over from the airport for about $1,600 roundtrip.

Please get back to me soon, so I can get you guys booked quick.

Thank you for taking care of Rick.

Aloha,
Sherry
Beach Vacations

I spend some time working on airfare options for Sam and my mom. Then I make a list of things that need to happen for the wedding and make notes next to the things that are handled, or need additional follow up. Rick is standing behind me and the cottage is getting dark. "Babe, are you working?" Shit.

"Not really, I had an email from your dad about wanting to fly over early and vacation, and Cross wanted me to set up his airfare and room for him. I checked on flights for Sam and my mom. Then I started a list of things that need to get done for the wedding. Too much?"

"Why don't we go for a sunset walk, sit with our feet in the pool and you can tell me all about the wedding stuff?" He smiles at me and pulls me up out of my chair to find I'm still naked. I giggle, pull my bikini on with shorts over it and I'm ready to go. Rick had already pulled his board shorts on and pulled a T-shirt on as we walked out the door. We walk over to the pool holding hands and get beach towels from the pool hut. I fold the towels to use them as cushions on the edge of the pool and take my shorts off before I sit down. I dangle my feet in the water while Rick takes his shirt off revealing his woman melting body to the world. He sits next to me on his towel and puts his arm around me. The water is inviting, not too warm and not too cold. He kisses me sweetly, "Talk to me about our wedding and our vacation and why you were working. Most important, what do I need to do to keep you from crying? I don't like you to cry."

I need to give him a real answer, but allow myself to get caught in the beauty of the sunset and everything that's surrounding us. Happy to be in my favorite place with the love of my life and getting married. A single tear trickles down my face and I consider jumping into the pool to hide it.

"I don't understand, my queen," Rick swipes his thumb across my cheek, wiping the tear away, "I need you to help me here. What am I doing wrong?"

"Nothing. You're perfect. I'm just happy and being a stupid girl that can't control her emotions." I gaze at him and another lone tear rolls.

"I like that you're a girl and you're not stupid. You are on the emotional side, but there's a lot going on. I get it. Tell me about tomorrow." Rick is trying to keep me distracted, and I think it's a good idea. I also think I should find a pregnancy test.

"I have a plan for us tomorrow! I want to take you to my favorite place for breakfast, then I want to take you out to Laie Point, and if the locals swap meet opens early enough I want to stop by there. After that, I want to take you to meet Malia and to Surfin' Shave Ice for a creamsicle. If we have time we can browse the galleries and do some beach hopping on the way back to the cottage. Oh! I want to stop at the grocery store on the way back to the cottage. Okay?" I gaze at him smiling with no tears in sight.

"Sounds great! So, what you're saying is you're the Vacation Commander tomorrow and I shouldn't interfere with the plan?"

"Yes!" I laugh and lean in to kiss him, taking us both into the pool instead. Rick tries to grab me underwater and I swim away before he can get me. He swims after me and we play in the pool, having fun like children. We both come up for air at the same time and he pulls me to him, kissing me with intent and then taking his mouth away.

"Tell me about the wedding stuff, my bride." Rick says while he holds me in the pool, not letting me go.

I'm distracted by the blue of his eyes. The reflection of the pool seems to add to their depth. "Wedding stuff. Alika has a couple Hawaiian customs handled for us. There will be a ring blessing and a Ti Leaf and Lava Rock Ceremony. It'll be nice to have the Hawaiian touches, since they're both positive things and we're getting married in Hawaii and it's my favorite place. Malia should have dresses for me to try on when we visit her tomorrow. We need to get you and Cross appropriate attire. I have a phone number to call about getting traditional Hawaiian Wedding Leis, leis for the wedding party and leis for the guests. We need to drive over to Honolulu to get a marriage license. I have the music handled. How about taking everyone to dinner afterwards or having cocktails at the ceremony sight immediately following the ceremony instead of having a reception?"

"You've been busy. I like it all. If it's what you want, I want it." He puts his forehead to mine and gives me a quick kiss.

I turn to Rick with a crinkle in my lip, "I'm concerned about one thing. I don't know how much everything's going to cost and I don't know if I'll have enough money."

"My queen, I love how you're thrifty and self-sufficient. Will you please not worry about the money? Let me take care of it. I want to pay for it. I want to give you everything you want. Think of it this way, there's no way it costs even half as much for our wedding here as it would for whatever we'd plan at home. I love you and I want this to be the way you want it. We're only doing this once, right?"

"No reason to do it again when you're married to the perfect man, like I will be." I smile so big it hurts and I kiss him. The sun is almost down and the music is playing at the pool bar. We dance around together in the pool with our arms around each other. We have the pool to ourselves and romance is swirling around us. We gaze at each other and my eyes turn warm, I feel like he can see into my heart and soul. I wonder if he feels the same and his expression tells me he can. He holds my face with his hands and kisses me wantonly until I wrap my legs around him. He takes us underwater and we continue making out until we have no more air. Rick picks me up out of the water and sits me on the edge of the pool, and wraps his towel around me. He pulls himself out and sits next to me shaking the water out of his hair like a dog, making me laugh. He stands up next to me and offers me his hand to get up. When he pulls me up I'm as light as a feather and get chills as the breeze hits me. He puts his arms around me and I get goosebumps. He pulls his T-shirt over his head, picks me up and carries me all the way back to our cottage.

We enter the cottage and he takes us directly to the shower, turning it on and letting it warm up while he peels my wet bikini off of me. He appreciates my hard nipples and stops what he's doing for a moment to kiss them. Rick pushes me toward the shower, "I'll be right there, baby," and disappears into the other room. I hear music come on and the volume go up until the bathroom is filled with Hawaiian music. A minute or so later Rick walks in, strips and joins me in the shower. He holds me to him tightly with his right hand wrapped around my back to my right shoulder and his left at the small of my back. His cheek leaned against the side of my forehead. Not kissing me. Not groping me. Not wanting sex. Simply holding me and loving me. I've never felt so loved and cherished. No words, only a slight sway with the music as the warm shower falls over us.

The water starts to cool and Rick turns off the shower. He gets the robes and wraps me in one, then puts the other on. He has candles lit around the room, especially by the couch facing out to the ocean and blankets sprawled on the couch. He leads me there and gets me settled on the couch, covering me with a blanket. I'm toasty all bundled up in the robe and soft quilt. Someone knocks at the door and Rick goes to handle it. He comes back with a pizza, macadamia nut cake, whipped cream, and a small box with a bow on it. He sets everything down on the coffee table and nestles in under the blanket with me. The light from the candles flicker about the room romantically. Rick holds me close as we watch the light of the night sky reflect off the ocean and listen to the thunder of the rolling waves as they crash at the shore. I'm warm and relaxed in his arms.

"I love you no matter what and I'll always take care of you." He talks into my hair, nuzzling me. "I know there's a lot of craziness going on and when I thought about it I realized I've turned your life upside down with my baseball world. None of that is as important to me as you are. I don't want you to take me the wrong way, but are you late?" Rick waits for me to answer, but I don't. I'm in my head dissecting what he's asking me. I don't pay attention, I just take my pill everyday and go about my life. I stop and try to figure out when Aunt Flo last visited, but I'm not sure. "Sherry?"

"I don't remember when I had my last one. Um, I don't keep track of it. It's never been a concern." I answer aware that my answer is unacceptable.

"How about I run over to the gift shop and buy a test, just in case you want it in the morning?"

"Okay, but I have a full day planned for us tomorrow."

Rick smiles at me as he gets up and pulls on his clothes, "I'll be right back. Do you want anything else?"

"Maybe chocolate syrup, if they have it." He shakes his head as he takes off out the door. I get my phone and call Sam.

"Hello?" she answers and sounds like I may have woken her up. Crap! Forgot about the time difference.

"Hi, sorry to wake you. Didn't remember the time difference."

"No problem. Is something wrong?"

"Just freaking out, nothing major. I've been being emotional and your brother asked me if I'm late. I actually don't know. I've never had to pay attention to that."

"Slow down, Sherry."

"I can't, he went to the gift shop to get a test and chocolate syrup and he'll be back quick. I need you to talk me through this." I'm slightly frantic while I try to maintain myself.

"You definitely need to do the test first thing in the morning. Most likely you're just stressed, but if nothing else you need to find out so the wondering doesn't add to your situation. You've been thrown head first into the professional sports world and now you're getting married while you're on vacation. I'm sure it's been a wild ride for you since you met my brother. Don't go thinking about it. The test is purely for factual purposes. Got it?" Sam gets it all out quick. Plain and simple.

"I can do that, but what about Rick? I don't want him getting hopeful and then... He's back, going to have to go pretty quick."

"Don't worry. He's a big boy. Remember it gives you two something to work on after you're married. It'll happen, you just don't know when." Sam teases me, but she's right.

"Thanks. Keep your eye out for dress pictures tomorrow."

"Goodnight," and Sam hangs up. Probably thinking I've lost my mind.

"Everything okay?" Rick asks as he comes in.

"Yeah, talking to Sam. I love your sister, can I keep her?"

"More like you're stuck with her once you marry me," Rick laughs and gives me a quick kiss as he joins me back on the couch. He digs into the pizza and I go straight for the cake. "Cake first?"

"Duh! I don't need pizza, I have cake!" I smile at him and shove a piece of macadamia nut cake into my mouth. It's delicious, sweet and crumbly.

Rick hands me the small box with the bow on it, "I saw this earlier when I was wandering around the hotel and I want you to have it."

I open the box to find a gold necklace with a tropical leaf charm hanging on it. Inside the box is a message that reads: Because you are as beautiful and unique as a tropical flower. Wear this everyday and remember what it feels like to be on vacation. It's delicate, and the leaf is organic and feminine. "I love it! Put it on me please." I hand it to Rick and he fastens it around my neck. "What do you think? Do you like it?"

"My queen, you're more beautiful than any tropical flower." Rick leans into me and kisses me tenderly. He gazes into my eyes as he leans back, "I really do love you more than anything, Sherry."

I'm not sure how I deserve this man. I turn my back to him

and lean up against him while I eat cake, and he devours the pizza. I guess he's the meal and I'm the dessert. I reach for the bowl of freshly whipped cream and he takes it from me, "It's not the same as the can, but I can make it work." He dips his finger in the bowl and comes out with a dollop of cream. I reach for his finger with my mouth and suck off the whipped cream, bringing a dirty glint to his eyes. I dip a piece of cake in the whipped cream and inhale it. He smiles at me, "We should save that for later," and puts the whipped cream back on the table.

We sit together quietly in the candlelit cottage, snuggling under the blankets on the couch while we listen to the waves crashing on the shore. The shoreline is only a matter of thirty feet away, yet it's like looking out into an empty blackness and only seeing the light of the night sky bounce off of it.

We kiss and eat whipped cream out of each others mouths, sucking it from our tongues. Touching each other and simply enjoying the time together with no away games in the near future and nothing forcing us to spend time apart.

CHAPTER EIGHT

I'm woken by a chill and the sun has broken, but there's a layer of clouds. The breeze blows in again and I realize I fell asleep lying on Rick on the couch. I carefully get up and close the door most of the way as quietly as I can. It's still early, but I have to pee. I pad to the bathroom silently and close the door. I find the pregnancy test sitting there waiting for me and Sam's words echo in my head. It's for factual purposes. Negative is okay, it just gives us something to work on after we're married. No need to get worked up or be upset. Okay, those are my words and I need to remember them. I pee on the stick and set it back down on the counter where I found it. I read the box to see what the directions say and wait for the facts to be told. I could get a false reading or not be pregnant enough for the test to pick it up. I walk out to admire Rick asleep on the couch, so handsome with his trimmed beard and muscular build. I can't help but smile knowing I'll always be with him, we'll always be together. I walk back into the bathroom to check the stick and it's negative, as it should be since I'm taking the pill everyday. I look at my pills and notice they're a different color during that time of the month, starting with yesterday. I take a picture of the test and throw it out. I may need to pick up another one in a few days. Somehow, I manage not to be upset.

I walk out to the couch and crawl up Rick, pulling the blankets up over us and placing my head on his chest where I can listen to his soothing heartbeat. He immediately wraps his arms around me and nuzzles his face into my hair.

A couple hours later I wake up in bed alone and hear Rick in the bathroom. He walks up to the bed and leans over me, "Are you ready to get up and take us on the day you have planned?"

I beam at him and nod. "Breakfast is the first stop." I jump up out of bed and quickly get dressed, pulling on a short Hawaiian print sundress with big red hibiscus flowers on it over my bikini and sliding my slippahs on. I fill my big purse with my wallet, camera, water, beach towel and sunscreen. I put my Seals baseball cap on and slide my sunglasses over my eyes. Then I stop and turn to Rick, "Ready?"

He focuses on me unsure, "Is there anything we need to talk about?" He's referring to the test and is probably confused because I'm pretty together this morning.

"Not really. Test was negative, but I checked my pills and I should've started yesterday. Probably not late enough for the test to be positive if I was pregnant. I'll get another test in a few days if I'm late." I smile and reconsider his heart, "Are you okay?"

Rick laughs, "If you're good, I'm good. It doesn't have to be right now." Obviously, happy I wasn't freaking out or crying. Rick pulls on a pair of khaki cargo shorts and his aloha shirt. "Let's go."

Alika is driving by in the golf cart right when we step outside and gives us a ride to the valet, calling ahead for us so the valet has our Jeep waiting. "Where are you two off to today?"

"Breakfast at Hidden Cafe, Laie Point, Kahuku Swap Meet, and then to Haleiwa for creamsicles at Surfin' Shave Ice and to meet a friend of mine at the North Shore Gift Shop. Some beach hopping in the middle." I spout off the itinerary I have planned.

"Oh, you got this down! Don't forget the resort has hula classes and ukulele classes if you want to learn. Need help with anything else? Anything new I should know about for the wedding?" He's with it.

"Nothing new. I'll check in with you later and give you an update." I catch Alika's eyes in the rearview mirror, not wanting to tell him about the guys from the Seals who will be joining us while Rick is there.

The valet pulls up our Jeep as we get there and we take off for the Hidden Cafe. It's about a twenty minute drive, but it's worth it for the best breakfast ever. We take a left out of the resort and drive Kamehameha Highway over to Laie turning right into a residential area, then drive most of the way around a traffic circle and find parking on a residential street. We walk a couple houses back and open the screened door of the Hidden Cafe to be greeted by the server from wherever she is in the small cafe "Aloha, sit where you want and get your own water." I agree this sounds odd, but it's this place and it works. The windows are glass shutters and screens, the tables are old and mismatched, and the walls are covered in sports memorabilia—mostly autographed photos from football players from the island, neighboring Kahuku High has produced a few professional football players and this area is into football as if it were Texas. I review the menu, but I already know what I want. The waitress walks up, "Long time, no see sistah. Welcome back! You want your usual?"

I look at her not believing she remembers my order, "Yep, passion orange juice and a beef stew omelette." Rick focuses on me and I order for him, "Give him the same please." Rick shakes his head at me.

"You got it. Your guy looks familiar. He play sports?"

Rick chimes in, "I'm the catcher for the San Diego Seals."

"I thought so! You should sign our wall after you eat. I'll get you the sharpie."

"What is this place?" Rick glares at me like I brought him into the twilight zone.

"Best breakfast on the face of the Earth. This is where the locals go. You're going to love it." The server brings us our juice and the taste of it makes me happy, a taste of Hawaii. We watch the locals come in to pick up food and hangout, talk story while we wait for our breakfast. The cooks and servers are all part of somebody's family and everybody knows everything, who their mom is, who they're dating, you want the scoop you come here. You can't help but smile in this atmosphere. Then the food gets to our table and the meal I've been craving for months is sitting in front of me. You're probably thinking the same thing that Rick did, Beef Stew Omelette? Yes! It's a big bowl of rice covered with chunky pieces of stewed beef, with huge pieces of carrot that make you wonder how they grow them, big chunks of potato, and some onion with the egg part of an omelette folded up on top of it. The stew is flavored with a touch of Polynesian flair and it's one of my favorite things. I cut through the omelette with my fork and spear a piece of stew. As I place the oversized bite in my mouth, it tastes better than I remember and I'm on my way to a food coma. I watch Rick go straight for the meat before trying the combo with the egg, "Do you like it?"

"What's not to like? Stew should be on every breakfast menu."

"Good! Tomorrow we should come back and split macadamia nut pancakes and macadamia nut french toast!" I laugh, I'd eat here everyday if I had the option. "Maybe the Loco Moco the next day."

Rick shakes his head and grins from ear to ear, "Whatever you want, my queen."

After breakfast we drive a couple miles to Laie Point and I

get my camera out, ready to tromp all over the sandstone terrain and get some photos. Rick meets me on my side of the Jeep, while I set up my camera. He reaches in to kiss me, standing between my legs and showing me his appreciation. He lifts me out of the Jeep. I wrap my legs and arms around him tightly, pressing my lips to his. His clear blue eyes reflect the sky and shine as he gazes at me. "Hi," he says simply.

"Hi," I say right back at him and smile coyly. I laugh nervously and I have no idea why.

"You love this place, and I mean this island. It makes you comfortable, playful. It suits you."

"I love the North Shore," I feel myself blush and I don't know why. "I've always fit in here, even though I'm a tourist. There's no place more beautiful and full of history, legends. This is Laie Point, the hole through the rock formation out there was caused by nature. Locals say it was created by one storm in one day, but there's also a legend about how the small islands got here." I give him a brain sucking kiss and slide down his body, "Watch where you walk." I take him by the hand and drag him with me all over the point taking photos like crazy. Taking advantage of a few opportunities to catch my Rick on film with the view. When I find the perfect place, I take a selfie of us together and try another using the timer on my camera. The ground is jagged and the sand can be slippery, but we manage to survive without injury. Rick parts from me while I take photos in other directions. I turn to find him and he has walked out to a cliff edge. He appears to be appreciating the wind in his face and the mist off the ocean. I take some more photos of him and realize I might enjoy taking photos of him more than I do the ocean. Wow. I walk back to the Jeep to send my pictures to the cloud and drink some water. I check out the photos with Rick and I love the selfie of us together, so I send it to him in a text with a heart emoji. Then I send it to Sam and my mom because they'll love it, too.

CHAPTER NINE

Rick hops into the Jeep, "Where to next, Vacation Commander?" He salutes me and waits for instruction.

"Kahuku Swap Meet," I direct him back to the highway and toward the resort, hoping the vendors are open. We pull up to the small group of tents and wander through checking everything out. I get two new sundresses, well one of them is more like a tube top with a skirt attached. Rick gets a pair of board shorts and an aloha shirt that matches my sundress. We watch the locals carving tikis and browse the Hawaiian wares.

We drive toward the resort and a part of me wants to make a sex stop, but there's no way we would leave the cottage for the rest of the day and we're going to see Malia this afternoon. We pass the turn for the resort and keep going. I have Rick turn off onto the dirt parking at Goat Island and park in the shade of the trees. We roll down the windows and relax, kicking our feet up on the dashboard. The breeze blows through and the sound of the ocean soothes me.

I take a minute to check my email and make sure I'm not missing anything. I have a couple of texts and emails.

Text from Mom - You two are good together. Great picture. I can see you're having a good time and well taken care of. See you soon!
Text from Sam - You two are adorable. It's gorgeous there! I want to go!

Sherry,

Let's go with option 2 and Lanai, but make it 4 days on Oahu and 3 days on Lanai. Is that an option?

Thanks,
MrSeno

I send a quick reply:

Mr Seno,

I'm sure I can make that work. I'll work up the details when I get back to my laptop later today and get it booked for you. I'll email your itinerary.

Aloha,
Sherry
Beach Vacations

Sherry,

The guys like the idea of the villa, but are worried they'll have to share beds. If you can verify they can have eight separate beds, we want the villa. Otherwise, book us four rooms. Set us up a car service from the airport and do what you can to get us all first class on the airfare. See attachment for names and info for the guys who are coming with me.

Thanks,
Chase

I think about it and I wonder if I can come up with a better travel option for the guys since they all want to go first class.

Chase,

I'm going to do some research for you and see if I can come up with something better. I'll email you details and itinerary later today.

Aloha,
Sherry
Beach Vacations

I send out an email to Alika to find out about the number of beds in the villa and I send an email to a charter service to get pricing to charter a whole airplane.

"Are you working again?" Rick is staring at me.

"Checking email real quick. Taking care of your Dad and Cross. This beach is great for wildlife. I've seen monk seals napping here." He gives me a look that tells me my diversion isn't working. "Shave ice or Malia at the gift shop next?"

"I have a better idea," Rick reaches for me and touches the

side of my face, softly running his fingers over my lips. He stretches across me and reclines my seat back as far as it will go, then reclines his own seat. This beach is almost empty other than us, and we're backed into a pretty secluded area. Rick rolls up the dark tinted windows most of the way and hangs my beach towel over the visors to block the windshield.

I'm out of breath with anticipation, "Shave Ice and Malia can wait."

Rick leans over me and claims my mouth with his greedily. Pure heat blazes in his eyes, "I need to have you, baby. Your whole attitude today turns me on."

I push him away and slide into the back seat. "Move over to the passenger seat." He glances at me funny, but goes along with my request. The passenger seat reclined to almost flat, Rick moved over effortlessly. My intent was to climb back over him and ride him, but I slide my bikini bottoms off in the backseat and admire him. I reach over him and kiss him upside down while I unbutton his cargo shorts and push them down enough to release his needy erection. I wrap my hand around him and stroke a few times, as I enjoy his lips and searching tongue. His tongue. I climb over him, running my hands over his body as I work my way down to his hard length. I lick his tip and take his cock in my mouth as he reaches up my dress to find me bare, spreading my legs and kissing me there. I suck on him gently and he tongues my sensitive center and folds, sucking and nibbling. Driving me to take him deeper in my mouth and suck on him harder, I lick his length and swirl my tongue around him. I suck on him and stroke him with my lips, dragging my tongue along his cock. His large hands are spread across my ass holding me where he wants me, driving me to the edge with his tongue buried in my sex. I grind against his tongue, but it's not what I really want, what he really wants. I slide back into the backseat and turn around. Rick slides a finger inside me as I do my best to back down his body and mount his rock solid dick. It pulls a cry out of me and Rick helps me into position. He puts the seat up part way and claims my mouth with his, each of us swallowing the others cries of passion. I ride him hard, my need matching his while he's seated as deep as he can get. I'm grinding against him and I'm out of control.

Rick reaches around me and pulls me tight to him, running his hands down my back. He whispers in my ear, "You say the sweetest things to me every morning before you even wake up. You empower me and make me truly feel like a king. You're the only person who can do that. I will do anything for you, everything if you'll only let me. I love you, Sherry. Let me take care of you." A stray tear rolls down my cheek and I don't know why. Rick wipes it away and kisses my cheek. He somehow manages to roll me underneath him and strokes into me long and slow, with his lips on mine kissing me, needing more. Suddenly I'm on the edge. I reach for Rick needing to have my hands on him. I dig my fingers into his shoulders as my orgasm hits me and all I can see are bursts of light. Rick's grasp on me tightens and he follows me over the edge. Our kiss is heated as he rides us through, both of us out of breath, hot and sweaty. He stops kissing me to catch his breath and leans his forehead to mine. "Baby, you drive me fuckin' crazy. I've never done anything like this with anyone else."

I giggle to myself, I haven't done hardly anything other than what I've done with him. I understand what he's saying, we get pulled in by sudden desire and need each other. We lose control and it doesn't matter where we are. I used to wonder if it was some type of reassurance, a need to make sure we're okay. But, it's simply sexual desire and sometimes it's a need to prove we love each other—we can't get close enough to each other.

Rick moves back to the driver's seat and buttons up his shorts. I reach in the backseat for my bikini bottoms and catch my flushed reflection in the mirror as I'm pulling them on. My hair is a mess. I dig in my bag hoping for a brush and get lucky. I brush out my hair and tie it up in a ponytail. I direct Rick towards Haleiwa, and he's the full definition of sexed up. "Ocean or beach shower?" We need to freshen up and we have extra clothes.

"I was thinking shave ice." Of course he was! He's always hungry after sex.

"Okay, beach shower it is." I direct Rick to drive to Haleiwa Beach Park. We park and I strip down to my bikini. Rick takes his shirt off. We run over to the beach showers and play, splashing each other, getting soaking wet. Then run back to the Jeep. I share my towel and we dry off as much as we can. I find my new sundress and pull it over my head. Rick puts his new shirt on and we match, even though it wasn't the plan. We're still wet and have wet spots on our clothes, but that's expected. This is the North Shore! At least we don't look and smell like sex.

CHAPTER TEN

We drive the short distance to Surfin' Shave Ice and get in the line that's wrapped around the building. I order a creamsicle which is shave ice with orange syrup and sweetened condensed milk. Rick orders a tropical which is ice with three tropical flavors of syrup, no condensed milk, no ice cream, no adzuki beans. As soon as he sees mine he knows he's made an error, so we share half and half after he promises we can come back and get another one while we are on vacation. We eat our shave ice in the parking lot, with the other patrons and the wandering wild chickens.

We get in the Jeep and drive back across the Rainbow Bridge to the gift shop, and find parking on the side street. We walk up to the shop and Malia is sitting outside relaxing with her mother.

"Hey girl! I've been waiting for you. Is this your man?" Malia makes eyes at me conveying he's a hottie. "Nice to meet you." She nods at Rick and wraps her arm around mine. "Come with me and see the dresses." She points at Rick, "You need to stay here. You can't see the dress. Browse around the shop, maybe you'll find something you like." Malia drags me into a room behind the shop where she has a makeshift dressing room set up with mirrors and dresses hanging up, waiting for me. "Your man is a good one, he has a pure heart. I can tell. You look different today. What changed? You're glowing? Probably just being a bride-to-be!"

I imagine myself in each of the dresses she has waiting for me and I'm immediately drawn to my wedding dress. "That one."

Malia laughs, "I knew it! Now, how about for your Maid of Honor? I like this one that's a little shorter, but only if it would be knee length. We can get it in any of these colors." She points to the other dresses hanging next to it. I consider Sam and which style would flatter her figure. Malia's right and I choose the one she suggested, I even prefer the traditional white and blue hibiscus print—It's Seals colors!

I take a quick picture of the dresses I have chosen and text them to Sam.

Text from Sam - You're going to be beautiful! I love how you're embracing the Hawaiian theme.
Text from Sam - I never look good in a dress, but that's the best I've seen as far as bridesmaid dresses go.
Text from Sam - What about Rick?
Text to Sam - White suit with a blue sash that matches your dress or white on white print sash that matches mine?
Text from Sam - White on white like you. Blue maybe for best man?
Text to Sam - Maybe aloha shirt for best man that matches your dress.
Text from Sam - I like that, too.

I turn to Malia, "I want these two exactly as they are. Can I try mine on?"

"Of course!" She closes the door behind us, so I can slip into it and it fits like it was made for me. "It's perfect for you. Beautiful bride." I carefully take it back off and hang it up.

"Can I get the Best Man an aloha shirt in the same print as the Maid of Honor dress? How about a sash for Rick that's the same as my dress?" I'm rattling on.

"Yes and yes. Good choices, too. What about shoes?" Malia wants to make sure I'm not forgetting anything.

"I'm thinking of getting a pedicure and going barefoot. Maybe wear an anklet."

"I like it. That fits your style and it's appropriate for a beach wedding. You should get French Manicure and French Pedicure, it'll be perfect!" I love how excited Malia is for me. "I'll keep the dresses, so everything is together and matches. My seamstress friend will make sure everything is perfect, wedding ready."

"What about a dress for Pia?"

"Already handled, just waiting to find out which print to make it in." Malia smiles at me. "No worries for you. This is right for you. He's the one. Be happy and love."

"Thank you, Malia. For everything." We go back to the gift shop to find Malia's sons talking baseball with Rick, and Rick texting. I walk up to him and place my hands on his cheeks pulling his face down for a quick kiss.

Rick smiles at me with a gleam in his eye, "Does that mean you found a wedding dress?"

"It means I love you. But, yes, I found a wedding dress and a dress for Sam and a shirt for Chase and..." I stop and turn to Malia, "What about an aloha shirt in the same material as my dress for Rick instead of a suit and sash?" I gaze up at Rick, "Do you have a preference?"

"I want whatever you want, baby. I don't care as long I get to marry you." Rick kisses my forehead.

Malia sighs, "Where did you come from? You're perfect for

her. Why wear a suit if you don't have to? I'll add the shirt to the order, but I need sizes for the men."

I watch Rick texting, "What are you doing? You never text."

"I'm having Cross bring me some Seals caps and photos, for these young men and the Hidden Cafe. He says large and I'm extra large." He truly is perfect.

"Don't leave out their sister." I turn to Malia, "How much money do I owe you for the dresses and everything?"

"Should be under $500, but I'll get you an exact price. She'll have it all in a nice garment bag for you, so you can keep your wedding dress in it afterwards." Malia admires us together, "You two are just too cute with the matching aloha print. You really do have a glow, he must be treating you right."

I thank Malia and buy a few things I need from her shop. Rick reaches to shake her hand, but she pulls him in for a hug and whispers something in his ear that makes him smile into his cheeks.

We get back in the Jeep and Rick focuses on me, "What else do we have to do for our wedding?"

"Get our marriage license in Honolulu, you and Cross need white pants, schedule salon services, finish up travel arrangements for our guests, we need wedding rings... I think that's it."

"I already have your wedding ring. So, you can finish the travel arrangements and schedule the salon for you and Sam tonight?" Rick takes out his phone and sends a text. "Cross will bring his white pants. Honolulu and a mall or something tomorrow, then we can lie on the beach for a few days? What do you think, my queen?"

"I'm behind!" I hear myself get whiney, "You have my ring and I don't have yours."

"Babe, I bought your wedding ring as a set with your engagement ring. I've had it for months." Rick pats me on the leg, "Do you need a vacation day tomorrow?"

I laugh at him because he knows as well as I do, I'm not going to relax until I have everything handled for our wedding. I can't imagine actually taking months to plan a wedding and inviting bunches of people, having a reception and everything. It would be nerve-racking! "Honolulu tomorrow. Stop at the grocery store on the way back to the cottage." He's learned his way around, and we take off for Kamehameha Highway.

CHAPTER ELEVEN

We walk into the grocery store, I pick up a basket and head straight for the refrigerator and freezer along the back wall of the store. Rick takes the basket from me and follows along, ready to carry for me. I pick up a jug of POG from the refrigerator, it's passion fruit, orange, and guava juice and more of a punch really. I walk over to the freezer in search of the local made macadamia nut ice cream. I pick up two pints and go back to the refrigerator case after a can of whipped cream. "Dinner and drinks in tonight, my king?"

"Perfect, my queen."

I pick up another jug of POG, a bottle of vodka, crackers, and cheese. Then I go to the deli counter and get the plate lunch family special with ribs, chicken, rice and macaroni salad. "Do you want anything else?"

"Yes, but it'll wait until we get to the cottage," Rick stares at me like I'm dinner and we head to the check out. I hand my kama'aina card to the checker and she keys in the code for locals. Rick pays before I can get my other card out, "It's date night."

We pull up to the valet and wander down the path to our

cottage. I manage to fill the mini-fridge and take a pint of macadamia nut ice cream with me to my laptop. "I'm going for a run while you work. Do you need anything?"

"If you see Alika, send him over. Can I use your credit card for Sam's travel? Also, I'd like to have a small Hawaiian Welcome Basket waiting in our parent's rooms when they check in, okay?"

"Use my credit card for anything you want. Yes, please cover everything for Sam and for your mom. Don't get cheap on them." He opens up the cottage to the gorgeous ocean view and kisses me with his don't-forget-me kiss as he runs out the door.

I check my email and get verification from Alika that the villa has eight separate beds if you include the fold out sofas and he adds a rollaway. Unfortunately, the estimate on the private charter is more than twice the cost of the first class airfare. I adjust the plans I have started for Mr. Seno and email him his itinerary along with my direct phone number. I also order a welcome basket to be delivered to their room on Lanai and send Mr. Seno an additional email with links to the resorts they will be staying at including the spa options, and Lanai Excursions website. I check first class airfare for the team again, trying to find a better option with enough seats left in first class for them all to fly together.

I send Cross a message on social media.

To @RookCross - Can you call me? Now would be great? Please and thank you!

Less than a minute later my phone rings, "Hello?"

"Hey, sweetheart. Do you miss me?" It's Chase.

"Of course I do! Hey, Rick is on a run and I have limited time without him in earshot. The villa has eight separate beds, but only if you count the two fold out sofas and a roll-away bed they can bring in. What do you think about that?"

"Book the rooms instead of the villa." Chase says without hesitation.

"Okay." I'm searching airfare while I'm on the call and get lucky, "For airfare I have found a flight with enough first class seats available, but they're not all next to each other. I'll contact the airline and try to get them to reassign seats. Best I've got unless you want to rent a vacation house away from the resort." I laugh and suddenly wish I hadn't offered a vacation house.

"The resort is where we want to be, please book us that airfare before it's gone. I'll text you my payment info. Hey, are you doing okay?" Chase is always looking out for us.

"I'm better than okay. Slightly stressed trying to get everything done quick for our wedding, so we can still have some vacation days. If I can book my mom on the flight with you, will you make sure she's okay? She doesn't usually travel by herself."

"Happy to be her escort. I'll pretend I'm her date. Just let me know."

"I appreciate you. If I can coordinate Sam arriving at the same time, I may get you all in the same car from the airport to the resort. You'll get an email with itineraries shortly. Thank you for everything!" I'm happy he's so easy.

"See you soon!" and he hangs up.

I purchase the airfare for the guys, book their rooms and call my mom.

"Hello?" my mom answers quickly.

"Hi, mom! I'm booking your travel. Is somebody coming with you?"

"Yes. Umm, the guy I'm dating wants to go with me. He already booked our airfare and a room at the resort. He said he's handling it and taking me on vacation. I'll be there the day before and we're staying for a week. Is that okay?" First time I've ever heard my mom say something to me questioning if it was okay. Weird.

I'm a bit shocked because I wasn't aware she was dating, "You're dating? I mean, I'm glad you're dating. You deserve a vacation. I'll see you when you get here. Do you want me to schedule a car to pick you up at the airport?"

"No, he rented a car. It's all taken care of. You take care of your wedding."

"Thank you. See you soon! Lots to get done!" and I hang up in slight shock.

I check flights for Sam and find one that flies in at almost the same time as the team. I send her the info to make sure the travel dates and times will work for her and she's good with it. I tell her she'll be meeting Chase to get a ride over to the resort and book her a room.

I review my checklist and Alika walks up to the lanai. "How can I help?"

We talk about the salon reservations and I update him on the additional guests, so he's prepared and Rick doesn't find out until they get here. I fill him in on some of the other details and make sure we are all on the same page. Everything is handled except the wedding ring for Rick and our marriage license.

I can finally breathe except I have no idea what kind of ring to get Rick. Should it match my ring? Should it be a more manly material? Should it be simple? My pint of ice cream is already half gone, so I stick it in the freezer and search the internet for men's wedding rings. None of them are right. After scouring webpages and webpages of rings, I find what I want. A polished, man-sized gold band with engraving on the inside. I need his size.

Text to Rick - Babe, can you stop at the jewelry store at the hotel and find out what size ring you wear on your left ring finger? Please. :)

My phone vibrates.

Text from Rick - I'll do it now. Just running up to the hotel.
Text from Rick - 12.5
Text from Rick - Want anything from the hotel?
Text to Rick - Just you... Do you like to make my phone vibrate?
Text from Rick - I'm going to make you vibrate
Text from Rick - On my way

CHAPTER TWELVE

I can't contain my smile.

I put away my laptop and set out dinner on the lanai along with a couple of POG-tinis. It's perfect timing for a lazy sunset dinner. Of course it is, it's date night.

I relax on a lounge chair, absorbing the view of the sunset, the breeze off the ocean, and the crashing waves. I close my eyes and embrace it all around me, the way the wind blows across my body leaves me relaxed. All of my worries have been blown away and the mist from the ocean touches me lightly, refreshing me. I sip my POG-tini and stare at the sky as it begins to change color, no longer the bright sunlit blue it starts to change to a dark orange with lavender clouds outlined by the shining yellow of the sun. The clouds look like zoo animals on parade with heart shaped balloons.

Rick joins me on the lounge chair, freshly showered, wet and shirtless. "Hi, baby." He kisses me with desire, pulls back and gazes into my eyes. I don't know what he's searching for or what he finds there. His expression changes from light and sexy to sincere, and I'm not sure what happened. "I'm worried that I pushed you and I don't want you to do anything you're not ready for."

I stop him, "The only thing that will make me happier than being with you, is being married to you. I'm ready for everything you have to give and I want to give you everything you want. Don't worry about me, I'm in this. I'm in love with you." I smile at him and watch his smile match mine. "Now, let's drink our POG-tinis and enjoy the sunset together. No more stress. No more worries. Just us together."

Rick takes my hand and kisses each of my fingers, he entwines his fingers with mine and holds my hand as we sit together enjoying where we are and each other.

We spend the evening drinking and grazing on dinner. I'm buzzed, maybe I'm drunk. I can't stop laughing. Rick keeps looking at me and shaking his head. "Why do you keep shaking your head?"

"I'm not. You're wasted." He laughs and he's at least buzzed. "I should get you to bed, baby."

"Woo Hoo! Take me, baby!" I yell out as he picks me up and carries me to the bed. I'm glad he picked me up because I'm not sure I could stand.

"Damn, baby! Are you kidding? You want sex?" I feel his hand against my breast and he wants it, too.

"Yes! Get the whipped cream!" I realize I'm being pretty loud and they can probably hear me outside.

"I don't think it's a good idea right now. Bad timing for that, but, my bride-to-be, I will not make you go without when you want it. I always want you." Rick closes up the cottage for the night, bringing in the leftovers and getting things put away.

I strip naked and climb under the blankets, while I wait for him. Within moments he climbs under the blankets with me and runs his hand up and down my body while he kisses me, sucking on my lower lip. I reach for his hard cock and guide him in. He moves slowly, in and out while he continues to kiss me, and I wrap my legs around him tightly, meeting him stroke for stroke. He touches my sensitive nub and instantly I'm lit up like a Christmas tree, crying out his name, "Oh, Rick! I'm yours my king!" He strokes into me harder and this is going to go quick, he's more drunk than he wants to admit. He takes my breasts in his hands and searches my eyes. "You want them, don't you?" He takes one in his mouth and sucks hard, biting at my nipple, while he squeezes the other. He licks and sucks while he continues moving inside me deliberately. Pulling as much of my breast as he can into his mouth while he sucks. It's tugging at my need and I suddenly explode, "Oh fuck! Hard, baby, hard!" He pounds into me making me scream and moves to suck at my other breast without breaking his timing. I arch into him as I scream and he's done with a low guttural groan, pulsating hard inside me.

He keeps stroking into me, "Fuck me, baby. You're perfect. I want more. Fuck, I need more of you." He pulls out and flips me over onto all fours. He smacks my ass causing me to cry out and spreads my knees. He explores my wet sex, sliding a finger in to find I'm still coming. He slams into me hard from behind and grips my hips, pulling me onto his cock, stroking himself with my body.

"You're amazing, my king, harder and bigger than ever before, so fucking huge inside me. I'm yours, my king. Oh fuck. Fuck me, fuck me, fuck me! Oh, Rick! Oh!" I scream out as my orgasm hits like never before and Rick follows in seconds. Collapsing and taking us both down to the bed.

He rolls off of me and pulls me over on top of him. "I love you, my queen," and I don't know which one of us was out first.

CHAPTER THIRTEEN

I wake up with Rick wrapped around me, still sleeping, and a raging headache. I pull the blanket up over my head and go back to sleep.

I smell coffee and wake up again to find water and aspirin waiting for me next to some coffee. I hear the shower turn off and Rick walks in to find me still naked. "Oh, what happened last night? You're all bruised."

I look at myself, hickeys all over my breasts. "You happened. I didn't know you were so much of a breast man."

"I'm a fan, but I don't leave marks." He glares at me with an evil grin.

"Try again." I wait for a better response and wish my head would stop pounding.

"Have I ever left marks? You must have fallen down when you were drunk last night." He's pushing his luck or my buttons, I don't know which.

"If you don't remember last night, maybe you were drunk." I tease him knowing he'll bite.

"You told me I'm fucking huge on the second round without

time to reload. No, I'm never forgetting that. Then you talking to me this morning in your sleep. I'm going to be walking around like the king of the world for days." He stares at me, like he wants to show me exactly how fucking huge he is right now.

"Just, no more marks until after we're married. I want no chance of any showing in our wedding pictures. Shit! I forgot about a photographer." I sit up straight and wide awake. "Taking me to the Hidden Cafe this morning? I need Loco Moco with runny eggs to recover."

"Aren't we going to Honolulu today for our license? It's the other direction."

"We can stop for breakfast on the way. This island isn't that big and it has more than one road. We can drive the other direction and then cut across the island. Different scenery." I take the aspirin and a big drink of water. I sit up and stand up slowly to test my hangover and I'll be able to maintain until I get food.

I shower quickly, tie my hair up in a knot, and dress in jean shorts and a tank top with my aloha shirt over it. I want to be county building appropriate since we're going to get our license today. I step into my slippahs, grab my bag and I'm ready to go.

I find Rick outside on the phone with his dad and take the opportunity to check my email and messages. Nothing needs my attention, so I ring Malia about a photographer and a jeweler, because she'll have a friend, she always has a friend. Rick is still on the phone and appears to be having a serious conversation.

I lie down on the bed and call Sam, going over everything with her and helping her pack. I text Cross letting him know my mom is handled and that Sam will be meeting them to ride over to the resort.

I close my eyes and relax while I wait for Rick.

Rick climbs in bed next to me and brushes my hair out of my face. "Baby, are you feeling okay? Are you ready to go?"

I look at the clock and I've been asleep for over an hour. My head feels better, I'm hungry and I feel like I could sleep all day. "I'm sleepy, but I'm hungry and ready. Is everything okay?"

Rick kisses me on the cheek, "I'll tell you about it on the way," he gets up and offers me his hand to pull me out of bed.

We take off for the Hidden Cafe and Rick finds it without direction. We split a Loco Moco and Mac Nut Pancakes. I keep getting up for water, probably drank five glasses. Next stop marriage license. We get back on Kamehameha Highway and drive 20 miles or so along the shore with beautiful ocean views, turning off onto the Likelike Highway into Honolulu. I use the GPS on my phone to fulfill my navigator duties and get us to the building where they issue the marriage licenses. We were in and out in less than 30 minutes, marriage license in hand. We get back to the Jeep and I offer up some ideas of places we could go while we're in Honolulu, "Do you want to go to Waikiki or drive up to the Puu Ualakaa State Wayside Park or go to Hanauma Bay or..."

Rick cuts me off, "I think we should just go back to the cottage. I think you need a nap, maybe on the beach in the sun. I will rub you down with suntan lotion and make sure you don't stay in the sun too long, basically be your cabana boy. How does that sound?"

"Only a stupid girl would turn that down," I gaze at him and smile because he's right. "So, did you decide not to tell me about the phone call or is it not important?"

Rick taps his fingers on the steering wheel, "I was talking with my Dad and we all know my mom isn't real happy I'm getting married, but she's been going along with it pretty well. Now, she says she's being left out of everything because she's not involved with the planning and my dad's idea to surprise her with an extended vacation backfired because it was all done before she knew about it."

"Let me guess, it didn't help that I'm the one who planned her vacation?" I try to come up with a way to include her without having to spend too much time with her. I don't want to give myself the chance to make it worse with my DOTM. "What if I call her and ask her to help me with something for the wedding?"

"What are you thinking?" Rick is unsure, but wants to hear it.

"Something that doesn't put her in the middle of everything here, but still needs to be done."

"I'm listening."

"What if we have her handle our wedding announcement? She can contact your hometown newspaper and the San Diego newspaper. She can even put together wedding announcements and send them out to family, friends, whoever makes her happy. She's on the proper side and these are proper things that I would probably forget about."

"I like it. But, you need to call and ask her to do it. Also, you need to let her know that I need to approve whatever she's doing before she does it. This way we can make sure she doesn't tell the world where and when we're getting married. She'll feel like I'm in charge and she'll like that. She's got it in her head I'm being controlled by an older woman. Before you say anything, I've never felt like you're older than me and I've always felt like we're equal. Everyone except my mom knows you're not taking advantage of me, my love."

"And, I'll send her some pictures of us together in case she wants them for the announcement."

Rick tosses me his phone, "Might as well get it over with. She'll answer if it's my number. I'm still her baby." He grins at me with a giggle and I call Mrs. Seno.

"Hi sweetie!" She sounds happy to get a call from her son, but I'm not him.

"Hi, Mrs. Seno. This is Sherry, Rick asked me to call you. Do you have a few minutes? I was hoping you might be able to help me."

"Oh, hi. Do you need money for his wedding ring or something?" I grimace at Rick, it's not going well already.

"No, no, nothing like that. The wedding plans have come together quickly, not requiring too much effort really. But, I thought you might be able to help me with announcements."

"What do you mean?" Mrs. Seno doesn't like me at all and seems to think I'm always trying to do something bad.

"Well, traditionally the newspapers in the hometown and current living locations are notified, so they can print a notice or article about it. I'm guessing they might want to do an article on it, possibly even with pictures because Rick is a professional athlete. Also, since we're getting married on such short notice I thought we should send out wedding announcements to our families and friends, maybe you could find something with a tropical theme, get them printed and sent out for us? We don't even have the addresses for everyone. It would mean so much to me, if you were involved with this. I want you to be part of our wedding and there isn't much to do since we're keeping it small." I added some gush at the end for affect and watched Rick shaking his head as I did it.

"Oh! Well, of course dear! I'd love to help."

"You know Rick is private, so he wants to approve whatever you're giving to the newspaper and the announcements before they're printed." I add like it's an afterthought.

"He's always been that way. I'll put it together and send it to him with the details. Thank you for putting together such a wonderful vacation plan for us, I can't wait to go to Lanai!"

"I was happy to, it's my specialty! If you don't mind, I'm going to take your number and send you some texts with pictures from our trip so far. Would you like to see a picture of my wedding dress and the dress Sam will be wearing?"

"I would love that, dear!"

I text Mrs. Seno the picture of Rick and I at Laie Point, as well as the picture of the dresses and I listen as they pop through on her phone.

"Those dresses are beautiful! Perfect for a beach wedding!" She's quiet for a second, "I haven't seen my baby boy as happy as he is in this picture since he was a child." I can hear her get choked up.

"Mrs. Seno, I promise I'm taking care of your son and I love him. I understand this is hard and I'm sure I'll feel the same when my child is getting married."

"Call me Brenda, dear. Did you just say you're giving me more grandchildren?"

"Well, we hope to give you at least one. Not necessarily right now, but soon."

"You can call me mom if you want or when you are ready. Welcome to the family, Sherry. So happy to have you!"

"Thank you, you don't know how much that means to me. Please keep in touch with me, you have my number. I appreciate everything, Brenda."

"Now, you go take care of my baby and enjoy your vacation," and she hung up.

Rick stares at me with a WTF expression. "It's all handled and I can call her mom now."

"You're amazing. Ten minutes on the phone and she loves you, plus she's handling announcements we probably should be doing." He shakes his head.

"Well, I did tell her we're going to give her a grandchild at some point."

"That would do it and it's the truth." Rick's attitude changes, "Should we stop and get you another test on the way back?"

"Yeah. About that, remember you asked me if I was late?"

"Yes."

"How late would I need to be before you think we should be concerned? I mean, how many days late would I need to be, to be considered late?"

"Sherry." Rick pulls over and parks. "Where are you going with this?"

"I'm just wondering, for my own knowledge. I could be a few days late or even longer from stressing out or something."

"Yea, I'm definitely stopping to get you another test." Rick locks his eyes with mine and holds my face with his hands. "Sherry, my queen, what day are you supposed to start?"

"Three days ago. I think. Based on my pills. The test I did was negative." I wait for Rick to process and respond.

Rick stops and focuses on me. It's obvious he's afraid to say the wrong thing.

"Babe, I don't want to get your hopes up. I don't want to let you down. I know this means something to you. Anything can happen and it could just be me whacked out due to stress or being on vacation or who knows what! I'm fine with it either way. Negative just means we have something we can work on later. Positive is unexpected and will make me happier than I've ever been because I get to give you something you want, something we both want."

Rick with his hands still on my face, leans in and kisses me, pressing his lips to mine and showing me how he feels about it without words. We're on the same page, but positive is better.

Rick pulls back out on the road and pulls into the next drugstore parking lot he sees. He leans over and gives me a quick kiss, "Do you want anything?" I shake my head. "I'll be right back." He goes into the store and comes back out less than ten minutes later with a bag. He climbs into the Jeep and hands me the bag. He pulls out onto the road and drives back to the cottage as I shuffle through the bag: Bottle of water, a couple candy bars, two different multi-pack boxes of pregnancy tests, and a tiny white T-shirt that has outlines of the Hawaiian Islands on it and says "Made in Hawaii". I pull my feet up and curl up in my seat, turning sideways to face Rick and leaning my head against my seat.

I'm woken up by the Jeep stopping and we're at the hotel. Rick walks around to my side and lifts me out of the Jeep, carrying me back to the cottage with my head against his chest.

CHAPTER FOURTEEN

We spend the next few days relaxing at the beach or on our lanai, ordering room service and eating at the hotel property restaurants (except for breakfast at the Hidden Cafe, of course) and being inseparable as we take calls and answer messages from friends and family. The warm sand is relaxing, giving me the feeling of warmth on both sides. Rick rubbing me down with lotion is amazing, his hands are so big and strong, yet a gentle caress across my body. The sun beating down on me, turning my skin a tropical golden brown unlike any tan I ever get at home. The ocean is a clear blue-green and you can see everything in the waves as they build and crash. The silhouettes of fish and sea turtles that look like they're trying to catch the wave like surfers. The surfers are out in full force with the current weather system, pipes are forming large enough to get all the way through and waves are hitting twenty feet in some areas along the North Shore. I'm enjoying the time and the personal time with Rick, the rubbing him down with suntan lotion and days of him not wearing a shirt. His hair is shaggy and he hasn't shaved in a week. I get a message from Sam and realize everybody will be getting here tomorrow. I've lost track of time simply lying on the beach with my man. I check with Malia and she has everything ready, including his ring. I check with Alika and everything is under control. I contact Brenda, she's loving Lanai and thanks me for the welcome basket.

I haven't started. I'm officially a week late. Rick hasn't said a word. The pregnancy test packages haven't been opened. Rick and I are sharing a lounge chair, he has his arm around my shoulders as we both lie there in the sun with our shades on, "I was thinking that maybe you should do a couple tests, my queen. It's a week, right?"

"Yes, it's a week. I'll do one of each kind first thing in the morning." Not wanting to get up and knowing they're more accurate at first pee.

"How about doing one of each of them for me now? You can do them in the morning, too." I get up and go to the bathroom, peeing on two sticks. I set them both on the counter and read the instructions on the boxes.

I hear Rick outside the bathroom door, "You can come in if you want." The door opens and he peeks in uncomfortably, not sure what to expect.

"What are you doing?" He stares at me and I think it's pretty obvious.

"Reading the boxes to find out how long to wait and what the different results mean."

"A plus sign is pretty obvious."

"Yes, it would be. But, it hasn't been long enough for the test to process and I need to make sure I give it long enough before I read the result."

"Sherry, what does two lines mean on the left one?"

"Umm, box says that's positive."

"Sherry! Will you look at your tests. My queen... We are pregnant!"

"Don't get excited. I'm only a week late and the tests could be wrong."

Rick runs his hand through his hair in frustration. He takes his phone out, sets it on speaker and calls Sam.

"Hello, baby brother. What's up?" Sam answers casually. "I'm kinda busy trying to get ready to go to Hawaii right now."

"Sam, you're on speaker with me and Sherry. Take your phone off of speaker." I hear her phone click off of speakerphone.

"Something wrong?"

"I don't think so, but Sherry and I have a question." Rick says very matter of factly.

"Shoot." I can hear the "oh crap what now" tone in her voice.

"Can a positive pregnancy test be a false result or only negatives?"

Sam takes a deep breath, "It's rare for a positive to be false. If you have a positive pregnancy test, you should take another one to be sure. Also, consider if you're late and how late. Things can change quickly when you're pregnant and you don't always stay pregnant. So, you probably want to keep it a secret until at least three months. Of course, you're never supposed to keep secrets from me, it's the law."

I take a picture of the tests and text it to Sam. "Do you see the picture I sent you?"

"Yes! I promise I won't say a word. I love you guys! Congrats! See you tomorrow!" and she hangs up.

Rick turns to me, "I love you, Sherry." He places his lips on mine sweetly, tasting me and cherishing me. He's overcome with emotion and it's his turn to have a stray tear fall. "I promise to give you and our baby everything you need." He holds me close and ginger, like he's afraid to hurt me.

"I'm not breakable, Rick. It's weird. We'll figure it all out together. I'm so happy to be pregnant with you and giving you something you've wanted for a long time. I promise to do my best to take care of us and stay pregnant. I love you, my king."

Rick picks me up and carries me back to the lounge chair, where we sit together with his arm around my shoulder. There's so much to think about, but I'm not letting it get to me. It's funny, for the first time in weeks I'm peaceful. I'm not stressing over anything. My world is how it's supposed to be.

CHAPTER FIFTEEN

I wake up the next morning to the sound of the crashing waves. The island smells fresh after a rainstorm hit last night. I'm cozy under the warm blankets with my head nuzzled into Rick's neck. He has the blankets pulled up to our heads, it did get a bit cold last night. Our legs are entangled and he has both of his hands on me as usual, but this morning one of them sits possessively on my belly. I take a deep breath and stretch, rolling over so I can see the ocean. His hand stays with me.

"Good morning, baby. Did you know we're getting married tomorrow?" Happiness bubbling in his voice.

"Yes, and everybody is getting here today."

"Do you know how happy you make me? This morning you were talking in your sleep and said the sweetest, funniest things. I almost want to tell you what you said." He never tells me what I say in my sleep.

"Go for it."

"Maybe part. You don't need to hear the sweet part, I think that's just for me."

"Spill it already." I wait, there's no way he actually tells me anything I said.

"You went on this rant in a sweet voice about how her name can't be Elle because it didn't happen in an elevator. You snowballed off into how it could be a boy and then about what should the name be and should it be Hawaiian or a family name. I can't wait to find out what you say next." Rick laughs and I can't believe he told me, but I can believe I said it. Totally sounds like one of my rambles, though I'm sure it was much longer and I asked tons of questions.

It's early and we won't get much alone time today, probably none until after the wedding. "So, what do you want to do this morning before everybody starts to get here? I need to go visit Malia to pick up dresses and stuff."

Rick kisses the back of my neck, "I have a great idea." His breath hot on my neck and his voice raspy sexy in my ear. He rolls me toward him and kisses my eyelids, then my nose and finally my lips. His tender lips and demanding tongue at odds with each other. He moves his hands to my hips and disappears under the blankets. He moves his hands over my body lovingly, as if he is memorizing it and kisses my inner thigh. He caresses my wet folds and I pull his mouth to mine. His hard cock against my leg, I suck his tongue into my mouth while I stroke him. I rub my sex against him and guide his cock to my entrance. He hesitates as he slides in slowly, he's amazing. His demeanor changes, "I love you, my queen." He takes my mouth with his softly, and moves against me slowly. The slow friction, and his mouth as it moves from my lips, to my neck and my collarbone. This must be what it feels like to be worshiped. "Is this okay?"

"It's wonderful. Don't worry, you aren't going to break me or hurt me. I get it." Offering him reassurance and he slides in further, moving a slight bit faster. I meet his strokes to bring him in all the way and I'm so full. He's exquisite. I massage his scalp with my fingers, playing with his hair and down his neck to explore the muscles in his shoulders. I wrap my legs around him and draw a low groan as he continues to move slowly. He squeezes my breasts, and kisses them, and it tugs at my sexual need.

"Wow, interesting." He squeezes my breasts again, then nibbles at my nipples. "Huh." Next he goes full on for my breasts, sucking and licking at my hard nipples. I cry out as I explode suddenly. "Fuck me. Oh," followed by a loud growl. Rick keeps moving slowly and wraps his arms around me tight, needing me next to him. Our hearts beating together strong and fast. He moves the hair from the side of my face with his nose, kisses me in front of my ear and whispers, "I don't know how I've gotten this lucky. Thank you, Sherry. I never want to be without you." That's all it took and the tears stream down my face, and I mean I flat out start bawling.

"Sorry." I grimace a smile out.

"Don't be sorry, now I understand why." He turns my face to him with his finger to my chin, "Never doubt my love for you." His eyes shine with sincerity. "Get ready and I'll take you to breakfast. We'll get some snuggle time later tonight." That's not what will happen because the guys from his team will be here and they'll be taking him from me for the night. He deserves it. I get up and pull on my bikini with white shorts over the bottoms and my aloha shirt to put on over my shoulders. Rick starts taking photos of me when I haven't even done anything with my hair yet. I run into the bathroom and brush out my hair, it's comforting down on my shoulders and I opt to leave it down today. I walk back into the room and Rick keeps taking photos of me. He grabs me, pulling me back down into bed and takes pictures of us together wrestling and kissing there.

We go to the Hidden Cafe for breakfast, today we order Beef Stew Omelets and enjoy talking with the waitresses. We stop at the Kahuku Swap Meet on the way back from breakfast and buy a bunch of North Shore T-shirts from the 5 for $20 guy. Rick talks to the carvers while I browse a couple other booths. He buys a tiki that means love and happiness, and looks like it's holding hands. The carver engraves it on the back with the date of our wedding and R+S.

I check flight statuses when we get back to the cottage and everybody is on time, Sam is actually running a few minutes early. I don't know which flight my mom is on. I expect everyone will be here in less than three hours. We take advantage of the end of our quiet time together and relax on our lanai under the tropical sun.

CHAPTER SIXTEEN

That moment when your concierge walks up to your lanai with your parents and finds you sleeping in your bikini with your shirtless husband-to-be, and his arms are around you protectively while you use him as your pillow. Alika knocks on the deck, "Hi!" comes out very loud. Rick and I both glare at him like WTF, dude? "These people were trying to find you. They say you aren't responding to their calls and you didn't answer when I called the cottage. They followed me over. I think you know them?"

Can you see my eyes rolling? Well, Rick did and turned my eyes away from our parents, so hopefully they missed it. Yes, our parents! Alika had a line up following him around the resort that couldn't fit in his golf cart! My mom, her guy, Brenda and Mr. Seno, who I've recently learned is Richard and no, Rick isn't a junior. (There's nothing junior about him!) Can you imagine the eyeful they all got? We've been in Hawaii relaxing for a week and have totally adapted to the lifestyle. I mean, who needs underwear when you can put on your swimsuit? A shirt? Not needed, I have my bikini top on. Even Rick has gotten down to board shorts and an aloha shirt he puts on when necessary, and doesn't usually button it. So, great that they all walked up and saw us lying there with Rick possessively palming my belly. They probably didn't think anything of it or even notice the detail, considering the visual they were getting. I'm not ready for this today and I know we're the ones who invited them here. I'm content to be where I am with my man and don't want to get up. Time to suck it up!

Rick saves me and sits up, pulling me with him. He puts on his huge happy grin, "I'm so happy you all made it. Sorry, about that. Naps on the lanai have become a habit." I reach under the lounge chair for my phone to check the time, and sure enough it's lit up with texts and missed calls.

Text from Mom - We just landed in Honolulu!
Text from Brenda - In our rental car and on our way to the North Shore! See you soon!
Text from Mom - We just got to the resort.
Text from Mom - Where are you?
Text from Malia - Called and didn't get you. I have the dresses etc. Are you picking them up today?
Text from Brenda - Checking in at the hotel.
Text from Brenda - What room are you in?
Text from Sam - Hey mama! Landed early and got lei'd! LOL! Where do I meet Chase for my ride? Hmm... That sounds dirty. I'd rather ride Kris Martin.
Text from Chase - Hey! Looking for Sam. Where is she meeting us?
Text from Chase - Never mind, she found Kris. smh
Text from Sam - I'm guessing you know about the team and Rick doesn't? It's a good surprise for me, too!
Text to Malia - Sorry! Coming to visit and pick up when Sam gets here. Going to bring the moms with me. More customers for you. ;) Expecting Sam soon.
Text to Sam - Sorry, fell asleep. All is well? Where are you?
Text from Malia - Perfect
Text from Sam - On a road and I can see the beach. I know, not helpful. Left airport about 20 minutes ago.
Text to Sam - You should take photos in the car, maybe a panoramic! LOL!

I stand and hug my mom, Richard and even a willing Brenda. "Thank you so much for joining us in Hawaii. Sam will be here in about 20 minutes. I thought the four of us ladies could drive into Haleiwa, pick up the dresses, do some shopping and maybe stop for shave ice." Rick stands and follows suit, but makes a face at my plan to leave him behind. "Babe, you can't see my dress." Besides, the San Diego Seals are about to take over this resort.

"Sounds lovely, dear." Brenda is the first to speak. My mom nods along.

"Alika, how about you show them around the resort and we'll meet you all in the lobby in about twenty minutes? Give us a chance to change." My eyes willing him, hoping he has an idea to keep them busy for a bit.

"You got it!" He turns and leads them down to the beach, telling them about the resort and leading them back to the hotel.

Rick and I go in to change, but he's ready to dig his heels in, "I should take you ladies into town."

"We'll be fine, babe. This island might as well be home for me, especially the North Shore." Rick gives me a new, concerned expression, "You can't be with me every second."

He kisses me and sighs, "I know, my queen. I should spend some time with my Dad. When is Cross getting here?"

"Cross is sharing a car with Sam, and they'll be here any time." I thumb through the clothes I have available and pull my white shorts back on over my bikini bottoms, then pull on my aloha shirt and leave it unbuttoned. I brush out my hair and tie it up in a knot. Rick pulls one of the cheap Hawaii T-shirts we bought out of the closet and puts it on with his board shorts. A more relaxed look for him. I love the contrast of his tan to the white of the shirt, as well as the way the shirt is at it's limit across his chest and around his thick upper arms.

Rick inspects me, "I'd be happier if you'd put a tank top or something on over your bikini top since I'm not going with you."

I shake my head, unsure what he's worried about. But, I appreciate his desire to protect me and switch the unbuttoned aloha shirt and bikini top for a bra and strapped tank top. "Better, my king?"

"Much. Thank you."

He takes my hand and we walk up to the main hotel, getting to the lobby at the same time as a stretched Hummer limousine pulls up and I'd bet money on who it is. The first person to step out is Sam, grabbing us and giving us a double hug. Next Cross steps out and shakes Rick's hand. "You two needed that much car to bring you over here? A little bit overkill, don't you think?"

Then the windows all roll down and the guys yell out "Surprise! Bachelor Party time tonight!" Rick walks to the Hummer and shakes hands with the guys hanging out the windows, clearly happy to have them here and approving of the gesture. He gazes at me knowingly as the guys unload and get checked in. He takes Sam's things, so she can take off with me and the moms, and checks her in to her room. Sam and Rick are communicating privately by text, I'm guessing he assigned her to be my babysitter.

The ladies and I take off, leaving the men behind and I fill Sam in on the plan. We stop to visit Malia and the moms shop, while Sam and I get the dresses, and everything else that Malia has for me. Rick's wedding ring is perfect. I get cash out to give Malia, to find Rick has added money to my wallet, $5,000 in cash to be exact.

While Sam is trying on her dress, Malia smiles at me, "Show me your hand." I hold out my left hand palm up. "It's a girl."

I stare at Malia in shock. "What are you talking about?"

"You're pregnant. It's a girl because you showed me your hand palm up. Didn't you know?"

"I found out yesterday, but haven't had it confirmed by a doctor or anything yet. Keeping it a secret for now, okay?" I gaze at Malia imploringly. "Rick knows."

"No worries. It's a good thing. She'll be loved."

I stop myself and ask, "How did you know?"

"I see it in your happiness and peaceful demeanor. You have a special shine to you. I thought I saw it before, but today I am sure." Malia hugs me, cupping the back of my head and whispers in my ear, "Everything will be fine. You will have no worries with this little one."

I'm at ease as we walk back to find the moms. Malia's words float through me and I believe every one of them to be true.

The ladies finish shopping and we load the dresses into the Jeep. I take them for Shave Ice and we wander Haleiwa, exploring the galleries and shops, before I drive us all back to the resort. We all get along well and it was an enjoyable trip, which wasn't expected. I never in a million years would've guessed my mom and Brenda would get along.

The moms go to spend time with their men, while Sam hangs out with me. We go to her room, so she can get unpacked and then to the cottage, to find out what's going on and relax for a few minutes.

Text to Rick - Back from Haleiwa. With Sam at the cottage.
Text from Rick - Is everything okay?
Text to Rick - Yes. Errands handled. Everyone got along.
Text to Rick - Having fun with the guys?

Interesting, no response.

Sam starts rattling out of nowhere, "I was thinking, I should stay here with you tonight. You shouldn't spend the night with Rick tonight. He should have to wait until the wedding tomorrow."

Before I can say anything, Rick is there with his hands on me, "No."

"Well okay then, baby brother. Where did you come from?" Sam says with an irritated older sister tone.

"Sherry said you were back and I wanted to see her. You have a spa and salon day with her all day tomorrow. Guys are all at the pool, talking about surfing lessons and how much we're going to drink tonight." I love how he just shows up, we've been together so much on vacation—I missed him.

Sam flips through the resort book, "Dude, you've got it bad. But, I guess that's okay since you're getting married tomorrow and sending me for a spa day. Hey, they have karaoke tonight in the bar."

"Karaoke? We should go while the guys are off doing whatever the guys are going to do!" Excited for something fun to do when I won't have my Rick.

"Better idea, I'll get the guys to go there and we can all hang out. My pregnant bride-to-be isn't going to a bar without me." There's some sibling communication happening that I don't understand and it's fine with me, it all sounds fun. Besides, I'm going to bed early and he'll catch up.

"Fun. I'll tell the moms, so they can join us. Please go play with your boys." I send him back to the pool.

Sam glares at me with wide eyes, "My brother is a handful! Talk about possessive!"

"Protective more than possessive. He wants me safe. I kind of like it." I correct Sam.

Text to moms - We are all going to karaoke tonight at the bar.

"Is there something we're doing here that we can't do at the pool?" Sam is stretching to get a view of the pool from the cottage. I'm guessing she wants to ogle Kris.

"No, let me change to my bikini," we walk over to the pool. I get another disapproving glance from Rick when I walk up to the pool. Apparently, my attire is somehow unacceptable. I guess I could've worn shorts or a cover up to the pool. Instead of worrying about it, I dive into the pool and swim to where Rick is sitting on the edge. Sam does the same thing, but swims up to Kris Martin. I'm beginning to wonder if there's something going on there. Sam and I play in the water, doing handstands and somersaults. Chase jumps in cannonball style to splash us, then has each of us hold one of his feet and takes us for a ride around the pool. This started something, but Rick jumps in the pool and claims me completely, finishing it before all the guys decide they need to outdo each other. The sexy scene Rick causes in the pool with me, my arms and legs wrapped around him, our bodies plastered together, kissing me deeply with his hands in my hair, gets a hooting and hollering reaction from everyone around the pool and some standing on their hotel room balconies.

Sam yells, "Get a room!"

Rick breaks our kiss and laughs happily, "I love you, baby." Then he whispers quietly in my ear, "I'm so happy to be marrying you tomorrow." I shiver, he goes into protection mode. "Going to shower and meet you guys at the bar in a bit." Nobody questions him, as he lifts me out of the pool wrapping his towel around me. He climbs out of the pool and takes my hand, leading me back to the cottage. He immediately turns on the warm shower to get me warmed up and it's just what I need. I get out of the shower, wrap a towel around my hair and put on my robe. I sit down on the couch to relax for a few minutes and watch the waves crash.

CHAPTER SEVENTEEN

"Babe," Rick is rubbing my shoulder to wake me up and I'm in bed, "The guys are all at the bar, you've been asleep for almost two hours. Sam is on her way, so you two can get ready together and meet us at the bar." He kisses me sweetly.

I don't remember how I got to the bed.

"Okay," but I don't even open my eyes.

"Sherry, are you okay?" Rick is worried about me.

"I'm fine, we didn't get our long afternoon nap today and I'm on the emotionally drained side." I open my eyes and gaze at him lovingly, his clear blue eyes focused on me. "I hope she has your eyes."

"She?"

"Malia said congrats and she will be loved." I probably sound like a fool. Rick furrows his brow, waiting for more. "As soon as I was alone with her in the back to get the dresses, she looked at me and told me congrats, it's a girl. She just knew. It sounds crazy, but Malia has never steered me wrong before."

"Huh, so you want our daughter to have my blue eyes and

she'll have your blonde hair. I'm going to jail for beating off the boys." He laughs as he turns to leave and runs into Sam coming in. "Good timing, sis. See you ladies in a bit. Sam, take care of her, she's tired. Love you, babe!" and he's gone to the bar.

I call across the room to Sam without getting up, "How was Martin?"

"Shut up!" Sam laughs, "Get up, so we can get ready."

"Better idea, get the ice cream from the freezer." Sam nods, then sits Indian style on the bed next to me with two spoons.

"OMG, this is the best ice cream ever!" Her eyes are big and she shovels a spoonful into her mouth. I laugh and try to get bites in between Sam's spoon. "So, are you ready for tomorrow?"

"Yes! Let's get ready, go eat at the bar, do some karaoke and go to bed early. We can go to breakfast in the morning and be back for our 11am spa appointments. I bet all of us who aren't hungover end up at breakfast." I laugh, Rick isn't willingly going to let me go to the Hidden Cafe without him.

"I like it." Sam gets the hanger of clothes she brought with her and starts to change. I drag my butt out of the warm bed and thumb through the few pieces I have in the closet. I slide the tube top sundress on with my lightweight sweater and slippahs. I put on the leaf necklace Rick bought for me and comb through my damp hair. Sam braids a few parts of my hair and puts it up in a chignon, so I don't have to blow dry it. It's loose and fancy. Sam changes into a short denim skirt with buttons up the front, a red tank top with a feminine ruffle collar, and leaves her hair down. We're both ready and find Alika waiting for us with his golf cart as we step out of the cottage. He was obviously sent to get us, didn't even ask where we're going.

Sam and I are the last to arrive at the bar. The parental units are all sitting together and in deep conversation. Rick and the team have spread out around a section of the bar, or I should say, they have taken over. Chase appears to be in charge, somehow leading the group to an organized state of drunkeness while they harass Rick as part of the bachelor party process. Chase meets us at the door, "My lady," and he bows to me as he takes my hand and leads me to Rick. Sam follows right behind me with a full belly laugh going.

I give Chase a hug and whisper in his ear, "I'm going to bed early, so you guys can have guy fun. You're in charge of getting him dressed and to the wedding at least fifteen minutes early. Not hungover, please. Sam and I are going to breakfast in the morning and spending the day at the spa. Got it?"

"Mission accepted." Chase salutes me, so I was probably being the Vacation Commander again. Then he whispers in my ear, "Being a bride agrees with you, you're glowing. Seno got lucky." He chuckles, "Are you sure you don't want to trade up?" Cross keeps it up because it bugs my Rick.

"Cross! Stop hitting on my woman." Rick is standing right there while all this is going on.

"I'm giving him instructions for tomorrow, my king." I kiss Rick solidly on the lips, taking control with my hands and my tongue. Then I turn and walk away with Sam to order food, and check out what the karaoke options are. He's watching me walk away, so I glance back at him quickly and wink like I'm sexy. He admires me full of happiness and we play a game with each other, flirting across the bar.

Sam and I sit next to the moms. We order a rib eye steak burger, garlic parmesan fries and a wedge salad, and share. I read through the list of songs and all I want to sing are love songs. I try to get my head straight, but it kind of makes sense. I have spent pretty much every waking (and sleeping) moment with my Rick for days, I just planned our wedding, and we're getting married tomorrow. I'm female and I picked up my wedding dress this afternoon. Besides, your brain would be sex-fried too, if you'd been spending afternoons napping in the sun with a shirtless hottie and getting sexed multiple times per day! I turn to Sam, "I'm going to need help here. My brain is in wedding mode. You pick for me." I push the list over to her and wait to find out what she chooses. Luckily, Sam asks me if I know songs before she submits them for me to sing. She also set us up to do a duet.

Little do I know, she submits for us to do multiple duets and nobody else is singing. We are first and this is going to be interesting singing "Islands In the Stream" by Kenny Rogers and Dolly Parton with Sam. We're also second to sing, luckily they start playing "Summer Nights" from *Grease*. It's a lot of fun and appears to be annoying the guys in the room.

The young guy on KJ duty calls me out by myself and Sam hunches her shoulders at me, not having anything to do with it. "So, yea, bra, I've been bribed to have Sherry do this next one. So, yea."

I hear the music load up and start to play for "Thinking Out Loud." My emotions hit me and I know singing this song will be the end of the night for me. I'm okay with that. Rick has been enjoying time with the team, but stops what he's doing and focuses all of his attention on me when he hears what song is coming on. My eyes focus on him, "This is the end of the night for me. I love you and can't wait to marry you tomorrow, King Seno." I watch Sam out of the corner of my eye, getting ready to leave with me as I start to sing the song. By the end of the song, Rick is on the stage with me and standing behind me with his arms around me, kissing my cheek and a stray tear is trickling down my face. Everyone claps at the end of the song and it quickly turns to clinking on glasses. Rick turns me to him and kisses me right there on the stage. I'm not talking about a quick peck or even the show from the pool earlier today. No, this is take me in his arms, hold me tight, claim my lips with his and dip me taking me off my feet and leaving me light-headed, an in-case-you-had-any-doubt-in-your-mind-you-belong-to-me-baby kiss. It should probably be given it's own classification, kiss doesn't seem to be enough. I guess I'm Seno'd.

Rick brings me back to my feet and embraces me, "Are you sure you're okay, baby?"

"Yes, I need extra sleep so I can be a beautiful bride for you tomorrow." I smile at him, "Besides, Sam and I are getting up early and going to the Hidden Cafe before our spa day starts. Have fun with the guys." I turn to Sam, "Let's go! I'm going to get you drunk on POG-tinis." She hops up and Alika's replacement is waiting at the bar door for us, it's like having my own personal golf cart driver.

Sam and I sit up, enjoying some girl talk. I ply her with POG-tinis, using up the vodka and we both fall asleep in the bed.

CHAPTER EIGHTEEN

I wake up in the morning with Rick wrapped around me, but today I'm squished between Rick and Sam in the bed. It hits me, it's my wedding day and I want out of bed. I kiss Rick on the nose, "Good morning, baby. I'm getting up and getting out. I love you and I'll meet you at sunset." I nudge at Sam, "Get up, get up, get up!" Until she finally moves, fine, I pushed her. Either way, we were up and getting ready for breakfast and the spa.

Sam enjoys her Hidden Cafe adventure. I order the macadamia nut french toast and make Sam get the beef stew omelet. She thinks I'm crazy, but comes around just like Rick. We talk with the Hidden Cafe ladies and warn them the Seals are in the area, since I suspect they'll be going there for food as soon as they're moving. Rick did have baseball caps and photos brought over for them.

We have some extra time, so I take Sam out to Laie Point. It's the place to be this morning. Peaceful, relaxing, surrounded by the ocean's strength and beauty. Almost meditative for me. It makes me centered. Sam and I take selfies, texting them to everybody and posting them on social media like fools.

Driving up to the valet, the resort van is waiting and baseball players are gathering.

Sam and I go directly to the spa and check in, to find we really do have a full day of spa treatments: manicures, pedicures, body wraps, massages, mud treatments, waxing, full hair treatment and styling, even make-up. Alika has made sure our dresses are here waiting for us and notified the stylist about the flowers that are being delivered. The receptionist directs us to a changing room and gives us assigned lockers to leave our things in. My locker has a really soft robe in it that's embroidered "Bride" and Sam has a robe embroidered "Maid of Honor". We also have boxes and cards left for us from Rick. He bought us white fresh water pearl jewelry sets to wear for the wedding. My card reads:

Sherry,

This is our special day and I want you to know that
you're special to me everyday. Married or not, I will love
you forever. See you at sunset, my queen.

Love,
Rick

I look up at Sam and she's crying after reading her card, "Is he always like this with you?"

I nod at her and join the tear fest. The poor young girl who's in charge of our spa day today walks in to find us because we're taking too long and has no clue what she's walking in on. The expression on her face says "it's going to be one of those days". Sam and I enjoy the day of pampering, relaxing oceanside between treatments and getting waited on with snacks, drinks, basically whatever we want. I'm sure that was explicit on our spa day reservation, I can see it: Give them everything they want and be at their beck and call.

Everyone is leaving me alone today. Malia checked in with me to let me know everything is as expected and she would be here later. No messages from moms. Only me and Sam, chilling out at the spa. That's not as good as napping on my shirtless man in the sun, but it works. I watch the sun in the sky out over the ocean and the time is getting closer as the sun turns down out of the high position. Alika stops in to check on us and tells me the flowers arrived, everything is as planned. I realize I don't have Rick's ring and message Cross to check on Rick and ask him to bring the ring for me.

Our attendant for the day escorts us to a private dressing room where they have everything hung up for us waiting. Our dresses are not elaborate wedding dresses, they are both pretty and perfect for a beach wedding. Sam's dress is a traditional hibiscus print in blue and white with a halter style top and a slight flounce to the knee length skirt. My wedding dress is white tropical printed flowers on white with a crisscrossing empire waist, a deep V-neck and hits me perfectly at tea-length. It's gathered at the shoulders and is perfectly fitted from the empire waist down. Looking at it on me now, I like it even better with my week worth of Hawaiian tan. I put on the freshwater pearls and they dance across my tanned skin. My French manicure and French pedicure are the perfect match. Only in Hawaii would a set of fresh water pearls come with a necklace, earrings, and anklet. My hair and make-up is already done, I need my flowers added to my hair and my bride's lei.

I watch the location of our vows quickly coming together. Chairs getting set up, Malia helping Pia get ready, Alika directing and supervising, flowers waiting on a table with a guest book, a photographer roaming about taking photos. Then I watch Cross walking towards everything with my Rick.

Rick is breathtaking, a gorgeous man in white linen pants and a white on white aloha shirt that matches the print of my dress. I have wanted him since the day I first saw him on the baseball field. I remember sitting in my seat and cheering for him when he didn't know who I was. I remember being distracted when I was simply within twenty feet of him and watching him do an on field interview. I remember the first touch of his hand and his lips on mine greedily for the first time and unexpected, when I met him at the Locale. I remember waking up the first morning after meeting him and finding him in my bed, wanting me. This man. This perfect man. And today, he's cleaned up, beard trimmed, freshly shaved and still has his grown out Hawaii hair, and a tan to match mine—because today he's marrying me. Our small group of guests start to show up and I watch as Malia greets each one of them individually, placing a lei on each of their shoulders and has Pia start playing as soon as the first guest arrives. The photographer starts by taking a video of Pia.

My quiet moment of observation is disturbed by a knock at the door, Cross walks in, "You're a gorgeous bride," he kisses my cheek carefully to not mess me up. "Here's Rick's ring. Can I do anything else?"

"Thank you. Stand by Rick. This is all because of you, Chase." It's true, Rick never would've met me if Chase hadn't encouraged him and put in a good word for me. Chase heads back to Rick. Sam and I watch, as soon as everyone is seated we make our way out of the spa and across the grass toward Rick.

As we approach my wedding guests, Malia makes eye contact with us and directs Sam to walk in front of me to her and for me to stay behind. The sunset is pink with orange hues, and I hear Pia playing and singing "Thinking Out Loud," it's perfect. I gaze forward as Rick turns and pores over me adoringly. His smile shines from every part of him. He has his green leafed lei on over his white and he's strikingly handsome. Malia stops Sam and places her lei over her head. As Sam walks to the front by Rick, Pia starts playing a ukulele version of the Wedding March and everyone stands as they turn to observe me walk down the aisle. I walk to Malia, "You're beautiful and will have a long, happy life together," she says as she places my lei on my shoulders and makes me wait a moment before completing the short walk to the beginning of the rest of my life.

The twenty-five feet between Rick and I feels like miles, he reaches for my hand as I approach and kisses it sweetly. We exchange leis while our Hawaiian minister defines aloha. Rick gazes into my eyes and nothing has ever been as right as this moment. The minister asks for the rings and performs a Hawaiian Ring Blessing with ocean water in a koa wood bowl and a Ti leaf. I'm missing everything and distracted, simply by the touch of Rick's hands holding mine. Rick turns to me, "Sherry, I knew you were the one for me the first night we met. I could feel it in my heart. I want nothing more than to spend the rest of my life with you. I promise to cherish you, love you, honor you, prove to you everyday that you're special, and fill your life with aloha just like you do for me." He slides the most beautiful wedding band on my ring finger. Gold to match my crown engagement ring, together it's a crown of jewels with channel set diamonds more than halfway around it and a round solitaire in the middle.

It's my turn and I gaze into Rick's eyes and say everything that's filling my heart with love for him, "You make my dreams come true. You've been in my life longer than I've been in yours, and it's beyond all reason. Good or bad, I'll always be with you wherever you are. You're not a baseball player, you're my love and I promise to cherish you, love you, honor you, give you myself whole-heartedly and to keep filling your life with aloha." I hold his ring up, so he can read the engraving on the inside with the date, R+S and the last line of "Thinking Out Loud," singing the line to him as I slide the ring on his finger.

The minister goes through the formalities and we both say, "I do." Rick pulls me to him dramatically, pressing his lips to mine and not in his don't-forget-me kiss way. He's confident, knowing we belong to each other and will always be together.

STAR CROSSED IN THE OUTFIELD

AN ALL ABOUT THE DIAMOND ROMANCE #4

Rookie Centerfielder, Chase Cross, flies across the field to make diving catches like a superhero. He's solid muscle, fast, tan, and has the drive to win.

Baseball players suck. I don't know why I'm attracted to them. They're not an option for me.

He doesn't listen. He's a distraction that will hurt me. I'm after my dream, not a man.

Chase the ball. Chase your dream. That's how I made it to the big leagues. Chase the girl had never crossed my mind. Chicks find me.

I'll do anything to be near her.

She's got me Star Crossed in the Outfield.

MUFFIN MAN

A STANDALONE NOVELLA

Robbi

"Everybody out!" The manager yells, running through the salon as we all ignore her. She's not the owner. Problem is the owner is out of town and she's in charge. She stops and at the top of her lungs, "Evacuate now! It's going to explode!"

The salon freezes instantly, the calm before the storm. There's a sudden frenzy of women gathering their necessities, and their clients as they run outside hysterically. I casually get up out of the salon chair and walk out with Deanna, my stylist, close behind me, and avoid the trampling stampede of frantic, high-pitched women.

We all gather outside for the details, but the manager is still in there! She comes running out with the massage therapists and their clients wrapped in robes. It triggers me to survey the scene for what stages of beautification we're all in. I mean, we all go to the salon for different things. Personally, it's how I stay blonde and that's not changing any time soon because I can prove blondes have more fun. The stylists are brushing out their hair, fixing their make-up, taking off aprons. I overhear what's happening and empathize for some of the poor women in the middle of getting services, when it hits me—I'm one of them.

The building had started to make a banging noise. The manager, Shawna, had taken it upon herself to find the problem. She was left in charge after all and the ship was not going to sink under her direction. This isn't some basic barbershop, this is Michelle's Salon and Shawna would not be responsible for damage to the custom European style decor Michelle has taken years to refine. It was the water heater. The water heater was making the loud noise, like it had air in the line or was trying to pass bad Chinese food. It was also emitting gas fumes and sparked every time there was a bang. The bangs were getting more frequent.

Which brings us to the bunch of women now standing outside in the shade of the building's front awning. It's almost lunchtime and the parking lot of the strip mall is starting to fill up with patrons to the food establishments, eyes peering at the motley crowd of women in smocks milling around helplessly. Shawna's on the phone with 911 trying to get, yes, you guessed it, the fire department.

911: What's your emergency?
Shawna: There's going to be a fire
911: Is there a fire now?
Shawna: No, not yet.
911: Sorry, we can't help you yet
click

At least, that's how I imagine it from the story Shawna told. There were others calling, it would be fine. Help would show up. Hopefully. Deanna, the only person I will let near my hair, is getting fidgety and twirling her soft brunette curls between her fingers. "I'm sure they'll be here quick. We still have ten minutes before we have to wash the bleach out of your hair. Everything will be fine." For those of you who are not salon savvy, leaving chemicals on your hair too long isn't good. Hair will break off, fall out, burn. I've seen it smoke. All kinds of horrible things, and I take pride in my long platinum blonde hair. So, let me translate what Deanna said: Ten minutes until utter disaster. Others have half a haircut, shampoo or conditioner in their hair, extensions partially tied in. The people who were getting massages are relaxed, even if their clothes are inside the building and they're outside wearing only a robe.

Everyone that could primp, had primped for the firemen to show up. It's a lineup and I can imagine the firemen walking the line, *"I'll take this one, and this one. You don't mind sharing, right?" The senior firefighter steps up and says, "Sorry, I get first choice. Seniority gets perks. I'll be taking this one from you."* Anyway, you get the idea. It's a beauty pageant and then there's me with a plastic bag on my head and a lady with foils sticking up off her head like she could receive radio transmission.

The sound of sirens fill the air as the long red ladder truck pulls into the parking lot, stopping in front of the salon. The important thing here is the possible fire, but I appreciate firemen as much as the next girl, maybe more. Definitely more. I love a hot guy, even on days like today when I only get to drool from a distance because I look like a bag lady compared to the stylists. The first guy is a bit older with short salt and pepper hair. He's fit and fills his navy blue uniform nicely. The second guy is shorter, still at least 5'9" and wearing one of those bulky yellow jackets with reflectors. His face is adorable, but the jacket hides everything else—not a hint of a single ab or muscular arm. The third reminds me of Goldilocks, he's just right. Thick, dirty blonde hair and the mustache to match. His navy blue uniform pants are topped with his station T-shirt which stretches across his chest and shoulders, yet loose where it's tucked into his Dickies. I'm busy imagining the things I could do to him. Naked. With my tongue. Deanna stomps her boots and drags me into the dog groomer next door.

"Firemen? Hot firemen?" I whined questioningly, not wanting to give up my view.

ABOUT THE AUTHOR

Naomi Springthorp is an emerging author. This is Naomi's third book and only the beginning of what she hopes is a long series of baseball romance. She's also writing other contemporary romance novels and novellas featuring firemen, Las Vegas, and more.

Naomi is a born and raised Southern California girl. She lives with her husband and her feline fur babies. She believes that life has a soundtrack and half of the year should be spent cheering for her favorite baseball team.

facebook.com/naomithewriter

twitter.com/naomithewriter

instagram.com/naomispringthorp

amazon.com/author/naomispringthorp

snapchat.com/add/naomithewriter

goodreads.com/naomithewriter

ALSO BY NAOMI SPRINGTHORP

All About the Diamond Romances

The Sweet Spot

King of Diamonds

Diamonds in Paradise, a novella

Star Crossed in the Outfield (February 2019)

Up to Bat (April 2019)

Watch for more info on these titles soon!

Betting on Love

Just a California Girl

Jacks!

Other novellas and standalone novels

Muffin Man, a novella (September 2018)

Confessions of an Online Junkie

Finally in Focus, a novella

25895445R00071

Made in the USA
Columbia, SC
08 September 2018